The Kingdom of Lies

H. Z. Syed

The Kingdom of Lies

For Laiba, Zara and Anika,

The Real Legends...

Chapter One

A baby bawls its heart out. The mother immediately responds to the little girl's cry and cradles her in her arms. The mother's beautiful, blonde, curly, messy hair hung in front of the baby's face. The baby's hair, however, did not happen to be blonde. Instead, it was white, which was perfectly normal for an Irene. Except that was just the hair at the front of her head. To be honest, the baby hadn't grown any hair at all—just one curly strand sitting alone on top of her head. Suddenly, a shout came from outside the nursery. "WHERE IS THAT DISGUSTING CREATURE!?"

 The young mother panicked. She covered the left side of the baby's face with an eye patch and quickly rushed to her husband's side. "What is it, William?" asked the young mother.

"Amber, my love, why do you care for such a… uh… that thing?" William pointed at the baby, his voice softer now. The baby was playing with its mother's hair. She took off the eye patch to reveal the most unsettling part of the unusual baby. Oh, I forgot to tell you. The baby, on the left side of its face, had a mark surrounding its eye. Like a burn mark, but how had it gotten there? The baby's eyes were also very unusual. The whole left side of her face was corrupted by the mark, and the eye seemed to be affected as well. The baby's left eye appeared to have an inky black iris with cat-like white pupils in the centre. The right eye seemed to have an all-white iris—the only thing distinguishing it from the sclera (the white of your eyes) was a faint greyish tint. A cat-like, black pupil stared up into her mother's eyes.

15 years later, Twylar Irene had become a middle child. Christie was born first— just one year before Twylar. Then, two years later, came Stacey, the youngest. Christie, Stacey and Sammy (a friend of Christie's) constantly bullied Twylar,

she shrugged it off whenever the subject popped up if she was talking to her mum. But the bullying was not the worst part. Everywhere Twylar went, she was accused of being a 'witch', or children would scream whenever she came close, and royal guards followed her everywhere so she couldn't practice her 'evil witchcraft'. Yes, her day-to-day everyday life wasn't the brightest there ever was. Not to mention, every tourist visiting the Isle of Irene pointing at her black burn mark and her peculiar hair. You could call it a peculiar case of natural two-tone hair, but others think she is a demon. Or maybe, if a wolf had eaten all the sheep, they would accuse her of being a werewolf. Well, they were rather stupid. Twylar possessed no magical power whatsoever, but they had guessed she was taking her time to develop some monstrous power to take down them all!

The Isle of Irene castle was mighty and massive. Light blue seemed to be the colour theme for the kingdom. The castle turrets were light blue, the doors were made of Luna Wood (which was light blue), and carvings of the first Irenes who founded the great kingdom were everywhere on the quartz pillars across the castle. Everything seemed perfect, but hidden away secretly was a crooked tower. It had a roof made of poorly crafted wood, a hole in the roof allowed rain and the cold to seep into Twylar's tower. The tower was on top of the castle but was so high that no one would suspect anything was there.

Now, why might a crooked tower with a hole in its roof be hidden away on top of the most beautiful castle man had ever built? Well, the answer is simple. That crooked tower is Twylar's bedroom. Well, once you manage the life-risking climb up to the roof of the second floor and manage to clamber into the tower, you will enter and see that the paint was falling off the walls, and the rug was half eaten by the moths. There is a small ladder leading up to Twylar's room, and once you climb up, there is a small wooden table with a chair and a single metal frame bed, a chest of drawers and a tiny closet. Well, the worst part is that Twylar's bed is directly under the hole in the roof, meaning the cold and rain will enter her tower and attack her in her sleep. Unless it's summer or spring, which is good because Twylar can sleep under the stars and watch the great silver coin in the sky illuminate the outline of her castle.

Twylar awoke to find her best friend, Ava Blossom, prod her forehead gently with a wooden stick. Well, not everyone thought Twylar was a demon. Amber (her mother), Moon Evers, Ava Blossom, and Lily Berret were the only ones who cared about her. They saw her for who she was, not what she looked like. "C'mon, don't worry about a royal guard following you everywhere. Did you forget? I'm a royal guard, too!" Ava waved her hand in front of Twylar's face, and she came plummeting back to Earth.

"THE DAY OUT WAS TODAY!????" realised Twylar as the brutal truth struck.

"Yes Twy, now go get dre— wait no, the king doesn't let you have any nice clothes…" wondered Ava, "You know what, Christie and Stacey aren't in their rooms, you can stea- BORROW some of their clothes" she concluded.

Ava was quite beautiful, she had black hair when she was younger, but she had dyed it into a lovely, light shade of blue. Her long hair was always tied in either plaits or ponytails, and a white bow was on top of her head. She was wearing the royal guard armour, except that the design was quite different from the usual.

A gold trim surrounded the edges. Ava was the best knight in all the Isle of Irene, which was why the king granted her special permission to accompany Twylar whenever she went outside. She's also chief commander of the royal army!

"Are ya done? We can't keep Moon waiting long — though Lily is probably applying last-minute lipstick…" giggled Ava as she looked out the hallway window — and, surprisingly, Lily *was* applying last-minute lipstick! Lily's skin was charcoal black, her curly black hair drooping over her shoulders. Her lips were glossier than pearls, and her eyelashes were heavily plastered with mascara. Originally of Nigerian descent, Lily always has some way or another to keep up with the latest fashion trends, even creating some herself! Moon is the daughter of world-wide famous Zoey Evers, she owns at least 37 restaurants in each part of the world! Even if someone was travelling through the desert, they would find one of Mrs Evers' restaurants waiting for them there. Moon's light brown hair was tied into pigtails, though she had dyed some light pink into it at the bottom, which faded into her natural hair colour. Her light green apron was covered with flour. She takes care of Sunset Café, one of the many restaurants Mrs Evers has opened. As soon as Twylar and Ava had come out of the great castle, they had officially started their day out. "Let's go to our normal spot, in Clover Cricket Central?" suggested Lily. The girls spent most of the morning just chatting, but Moon had offered to open Sunset Café early so that they could get some breakfast.

"MMMMMM", sighed Ava, gobbling up her sausages greedily; she was done with her breakfast, soon followed by the rest.

"Moon, your cooking skills are unmatched!" complimented Twylar as she handed her dirty plate to one of the other terrified workers.

"Miss Moon? I quit!" he squealed as he dropped Twylar's plate and sped out of the café. Pretending she hadn't witnessed anything, she stepped outside into the sunshine, but the children playing in the park stopped breathing. One of them pointed at Twylar. They screamed and ran off to their mothers, who threw dirty looks at her. Feeling ashamed, Twylar covered her left eye and pulled her hood on.

"Ignore them, Twy, they're just stupid, no-life, brain empty, worthless—" Ava continued ranting on until she finally came to an end, "Idiots!" she finally concluded, after saying her long list of insulting words.

Lily put her hand on Twylar's shoulder, *"Why should I care what they think of me..."* thought Twylar bravely. Soon, she forgot about that incident and headed happily towards Clover Cricket Cinema. The good thing about being feared is that you get free tickets and entries to about anywhere you want to go! Though, that's the only good side to it. As they walked over to the cinema, they could see something... something laughing and pointing... at Twylar.

Christie laughed savagely as Twylar came towards them, "What do you want?" asked Moon, standing in front of Twylar. Sammy shoved her out of the way. The ferocious girl had hazel eyes and light brown hair, her face was stuck permanently on a frown, and she was one of the many people who made Twylar's life hell. Let me give you some examples. When Twylar was mopping the floors, Sammy purposely spilt her drink on the floor and smashed the glass with her foot. And as if that's not bad enough, Sammy also destroyed King William's portrait and blamed it entirely on Twylar! (Which, as a punishment, she had to watch the new painting of her dad dry. She wasn't allowed to move from her exact spot until the paint had dried!)

Ava glared at Sammy as Moon fell to the ground, her face was bleeding. Twylar shoved Sammy back, but the psychopath just smiled. Stacey let out a high-pitched shriek of laughter.

"Pfffft! finally standing up for yourself 'Twy?" Christie laughed.

"HEY! Only my BEST friends can call me that!" said Twylar angrily.

"Aww, is the little baby upset about a simple joke?" Stacey died of laughter.

"And does Shrek's daughter have maximum ugliness as always?" Stacey stopped laughing.

"You're calling mum Shrek. She won't like that now, would she?" said Christie coolly.

"I'm so sorry, my dear sister, but is Mum a boy? No. And did I just run a DNA test saying you're adopted? Yes," replied Twylar.

Sammy pulled out her fists menacingly, while Stacey pulled out her phone, meaning she was threatening to tell dad.

"If anything, you're adopted! You look nothing like Mum or Dad. Anyways, say you're sorry, or Stacey's gonna tell Dad." Instructed Christie.

"Well, Mum told me to never lie, so I can't say sorry to you!" snapped Twylar.

"You know what, Stacey, don't tell Dad. I'm going to show society how evil you really are, you demon!" yelled Christie. She picked up her long, light blue dress and rushed off towards the park. "EVERYONE, IT IS ME! CHRISTIE!!!" announced Christie. Everyone turned towards her and cheered.

"Thank you for giving me money, dear princess!" shouted a random homeless man, "WE LOVE YOU, PRINCESS CHRISTIE!!" screamed the audience.

"I WOULD LIKE TO SAY SOMETHING ABOUT MY EVIL SISTER," everyone held their breath. "TODAY WHILST ME AND MY SISTER WENT OUT, TWYLAR CAME AND PUSHED STACEY TO THE GROUND!!" lied Christie, "HER FACE WAS BLEEDING, COME HERE STACEY!" commanded Christie. Stacey obediently walked over to the stage Christie was standing on.

Stacey's face was covered in red paint. She tried to fake cry, but she couldn't hide her smirk. The audience gasped, taking in every ounce of Christie's lies. "SEE WHAT THAT DEMON DID TO MY SISTER!" ranted Christie.

But suddenly, the audience parted and let through the queen of the Isle of Irene, "What is this, Christina Irene!?" demanded Amber, their mother. Her gorgeous eyes had turned to flame as she knew what Christie had attempted to do.

"Nothing, Mother..." mumbled Christie as she ran away.

"Everyone, go back to doing what you were doing!" announced Amber. Everyone turned their heads back round.

"My dear child, what exactly did you say to Christina?" asked Amber as she hugged her daughter.

"Uhm, I might've said she's adopted, but nothing much!" muttered Twylar as she scrambled to get out of her mother's clutches.

"My queen, I'm sorry for not protecting your daughter, Sammy wouldn't let me through!" complained Ava,

"Oh, it's fine, my dear, you've done enough by just being Twylar's friend!" smiled Amber as she trotted off towards the cinema, gave the receptionist a warm smile and bought four tickets. "Here, go watch your favourite movie, sweeties!" Amber walked out and headed towards the castle. The girls were overjoyed, but Twylar was most grateful. Her mother had just saved her from a month's worth of chores!

As they headed to the room where the movie was playing, Twylar caught hold of a voice, a voice sounding shrill and inhumane. *"Chop down the tree..."* it muttered quietly. Twylar tried to ignore it and looked around, but it almost seemed as if the voice knew. *"CHOP DOWN THE TREE!!"* it screamed. Twylar jumped and looked around. *"Someone must be playing a prank on me... well, that's obviously true; everyone hates me."* Thought Twylar savagely. Soon, she found herself drowning in a sea of thoughts.

"WHERE IS THAT DISGUSTING CREATURE!??"

"Dad? Why can't I go outside?"

"Pfft finally standing up for yourself, 'Twy?'"

Twylar fell to the ground, her head having full impact on the floor.

"Twy? TWY!" yelled Lily as she shook Twylar awake. She stared at her surroundings, which she immediately recognized as Lily's cottage. The thick forest surrounding the small cottage was armed with thorns and poisonous berry bushes, which was good security as Lily's home was right in the middle of it. Only God knows how Lily, Moon and Ava managed it through whilst also carrying Twylar. The inside of the cottage was giving off a very homely, cosy vibe. Hanging potted plants hung from every corner of the room, and a fireplace was lit with a rocking chair beside it. A small ladder led to Lily's room (which Twylar was in right now). She was lying in Lily's bed, looking up at two worried faces peering down on her. "Twy, why'd you faint? Luckily, I was able to make some soup with the things Lily has in her fridge..." asked Moon, bringing up a small table and putting down the soup on it.

"Well, why did you faint?" repeated Moon as she sat down beside Twylar.

"Well, I heard a voice and..." began Twylar.

"You know, hearing voices is the first sign of madness." Stated Lily as though she knew everything.

"Well, what did the voices say?" urged Moon eagerly.

"It said 'chop down the?" began Twylar again before getting distracted. "Ava, can you open the window?" asked Twylar. Ava did as she was asked and opened the window. Outside was an envelope sealed carefully and addressed to...

"Me!?" wondered Twylar aloud. Twylar threw it into the fire, thinking that it was another hate letter from one of the civilians. But, if it was, how could it have flown here? Normal civilians can't do magic...

"Well, I'll take you back to your tower, you need rest! And you can't stay at Lily's, cuz where will she sleep?" asked Ava as she dragged Twylar out the bed.

"Well, goodnight, guys! Ava, text me when Twy gets home kay?" sighed Moon. Once she reached her crooked tower, she jumped right onto her bed. She stared up at the starry sky, but unluckily, it had started to rain. Twylar decided to sleep on the floor tonight, as she was NOT going to get wet tonight.

When she woke up, she climbed down the ladders to see a small purple book and a note on the table. The note said: "Dear Twylar Irene, it's me, your mother. I have gone on a trip to Dragon Thorn to meet their Queen, so stay safe and don't let Stacey and Christina get to you!

P. S. The purple book on the table is a gift from me, enjoy your new diary!"

Twylar was excited to write in her diary, it had a big gem on the cover, an amethyst, it was called. The book had a light purple, leathery kind of cover, and its pages smelt fresh.

Twylar had no time to waste; she could go to the castle cafeteria, but the lunch lady didn't like her much after she stole a piece of chicken! Luckily, someone called Moon existed. Twylar hurried into her cleaning costume, grabbed her supplies and made sure to catch her eye patch. She clumsily pulled it over her face and pulled on her hoodie over the outfit. Ava, of course, had to go outside with Twylar, and they both ran off to Sunset café. Once they came in, the customers took one look at Twylar and panicked before then settling their eyes on Ava and realising they were safe.

Moon sat them down at their Favourite spot, and asked what they would like to eat. "Just the usual Moon, except this time I'd like some strawberry boba," asked Twylar, staring anxiously at the customers who were staring back at her.

"Hmm, maybe just one whole English breakfast?" suggested Ava.

"Without the hashbrowns, those make me gag." Moon smiled warmly and headed off to the kitchen to make their orders. As they waited, a man with wild, messy hair approached them.

"Hey, you. The one with the weird hair, not you, the demon.," he said harshly. Ava pointed to herself questioningly.

"Uhm, that would be me?" asked Twylar innocently.

"Hah! I knew you were a demon, those eyes and that black burn mark too!" he laughed. "Just go back to hell, nobody wants you here!" He said bitterly, and walked off towards the counter, handed Moon a few pennies for his meal, and left.

"Ugh, who does he think he is?" snorted Ava, as she threw a lethal look at him walking down the street.

Twylar's mood had changed profoundly since the talk with that rude dude. She seemed 'too sick' to do her chores, but it was just Twylar thinking about life questions. *"Why aren't I normal?" "Why did God create me this way? Why me?"*

Her mind was racing now. "Why do I have different hair and eyes? Am I actually a demon?"

There was no stopping the thoughts from bursting into her mind. *"Why can't people just accept me?"*

Her mind was on another planet now.

Suddenly, her life-questioning thoughts were interrupted by the same shrill voice she heard at the cinema. Twylar immediately whipped her head around, but no one was there whispering into her ear. *"I know."* It whispered. *"I know why you were born this way."* The air was filled with lingering tension. And Twylar was silently urging the voice to go on. *"truthfully, I don't know. Only God does."* Twylar let out an audible sigh. *"don't be so disappointed! I do have some ideas why you're like this."* Twylar held her breath. *"Well, I was lying. I honestly don't know why you're like this, I was trying to cheer you up."* Twylar sighed again. There was no hope. That was the one important thing Twylar had learned while growing up. Suddenly, an old memory flashed in front of her eyes.

Twylar was 2 years old, she had a full head of hair, and she was playing with a toy car. "Voom! Voom!" she babbled, playfully crashing the car into various objects. Suddenly, Christie came towards her. Christie was about 3 at that time, and she smacked the car out of Twylar's hand. She laughed bitterly. But Twylar did not care and hung her head low. Tomorrow would be Twylar's birthday! She was so excited! She ran to the kitchen, and sure enough, there was one huge package. Amber stood in the corner, it was kind of suspicious for William to suddenly give Twylar gifts after being mean and all that.

William picked up Twylar (with a disgusted face) he dropped her on the table and immediately went to wash his hands. The innocent child ripped open the packaging, only to find a dead mouse. A real dead mouse—caught by the local rat catcher. Twylar screamed and jumped off the table. Being only 2 (my mistake, seeing as it's her birthday, I mean 3), it was a high jump from the table to the ground, so she fell flat on her face. Her forehead was bleeding like mad, but strangely, she wasn't crying. All throughout Twylar's childhood, she had learned never to have hope. It simply wasn't possible that her dad would come up to her and apologize. Christie, Stacey and Sammy, too!

Chapter Two

The next day dawned, and Twylar was already so tired moments after waking up, *"Must be all the chores, Stacey did come walking in the castle with muddy shoes on PURPOSE!!"* thought Twylar angrily. She got ready, only to realise she had a day off today. She changed into the clothes she'd stolen from Christie and walked out of her tower. She held on to the tiles of the roof and began to clamber down. She opened one of the windows of the other towers a few feet down and made her way to the castle gates. Ava was waiting for her near checkout and signed Twylar out (which meant she'd gone outside with a guard).

The girls met up at the usual Clover Lily Central.

"Guys should we make a name for our friend group?" suggested Moon. The girls all voted names for their group name, but 'The Legends' got 3 votes and 'Demon Gang' got one.

"Well, guess our friend group name is 'The Legends'!" exclaimed Ava cheerfully.

"Lily, do you mind if we come over to your cottage? It's way more cosy than this park!" pleaded Twylar, stealing glances at all the disgusted faces looking her way.

Lily agreed, and they navigated slowly towards her cottage, Moon's clothes got ripped by some of the thorns, but she insisted she was fine; Ava lost her white bow, and Lily made it through untouched. Twylar was the only one who realised you could just climb up the trees and swing from vine to branch like a monkey, though she did get a bit of mud on her clothes!

When they finally made it to Lily's cottage, she welcomed them inside and they took a seat by the roaring fire. Lily was making hot chocolate in the kitchen whilst Twylar told of what the voice had said a day ago.

"Well, at least we know the voice isn't dangerous," concluded Moon.

"But who knows, it might be evil!" smirked Ava.

"Oh shut it guys..." snapped Twylar as she was becoming more and more anxious about the voice. And, right on cue, the voice tuned in to her thoughts. *"Trust me, I'm not evil!"* reassured the voice. Twylar jumped. She whipped her head round to see if anyone was whispering in her ear- *"it's obvious no one's whispering to you, learn from last time."* Twylar ignored it and drank her hot chocolate. *"ohh so you're ignoring me huh? Well guess what I have complete access to all your memories!"* it half-shouted, half-screamed. *"so?"* thought Twylar back. *"that means I can replay your worst memories, like last time!"*

Suddenly, true to the voice's words, Twylar remembered an old but horrible memory of her childhood. She was in primary school. Her sisters were in boarding schools all the way in Evergreen, whilst Twylar was stuck with Sammy in Woden Hills primary school. Everyone was scared of her, but one of the royal guards was with her to make sure she couldn't do anything "evil" King William decided that Christie and Stacey should move to Woden Hills, so they moved schools. Twylar was kind of enjoying the absence of Christie and Stacey, but now that was going to end. First, she had Sammy to deal with, and now this!

Everyone cheered as the two beloved princesses entered the room. While everyone was wearing their school uniforms, Christie was wearing a light blue dress, and a simple, gold tiara sat upon her white hair. All Irenes have white hair; the only exception is Amber, their mother. But the folks don't really care, as long as her hair isn't black! See, years ago, an Irene called 'Camilla Rosemary Irene' had black hair and serpent-green eyes; everyone loved her, but her brother, 'William Chelsea Irene' was even more loved. He was thought to be an angel sent down from the heavens, but he was nothing like an angel. He was the opposite of his sister, he did bad deeds but blamed it on poor Camilla. But even so, people still loved her. So William decided to do something that would make the Isle of Irene turn its back on her...

That's when the war started. Because of that evil plan, William made it look like Camilla was evil when he was the real culprit. All of the royal guards fought bravely against her, but Camilla was saved. She was saved by a witch, as the story goes, but the witch had made her into a hideous horse. A very powerful, hideous horse. She can turn back into a human and on the final day, in the last battle, even with the powers the witch had gifted her, William had won. He turned her into a statue of stone, using a powerful weapon, a weapon which would make sure Camilla would never break free from her stony prison.

Now, everyone thought people with black hair were either demons or minions of Camilla, trying to break her free on the outside. And unluckily for Twylar, she had black hair. The people didn't care if the front of her hair was white, they didn't care if her hair was two-tone, they wouldn't care if the world was burning right before their eyes! Twylar slumped in her seat, the guard who was standing next to her seemed as if he was regretting his life decisions. He snorted in disgust. During a break, Sammy, joined by Christie and Stacey, came waddling over to the bench Twylar was sitting at. "Why can't you just leave me alone, you fat pigs!?" shouted Twylar. Everyone in the playground stopped and stared. Twylar fell silent, feeling a bit more alert of everyone staring at her. She quietly said sorry and ran off. She could hear them all laughing as she ran out; the guard who was supposed to be following her laughed with them. He wiped a tear from his eyes.

Even in lunch, Twylar wasn't safe! Twylar came back to her senses. Her friends were staring at her. "Lemme guess.. the voice?" guessed Lily, staring suspiciously at Twylar. "Obviously, apparently, it can make me remember old memories." Shivered Twylar. "It definitely is evil.. it made me remember an old-school memory!" Twylar was now in high school, year 11. She walked to school the following day, but it was... "CANCELLED!?" screamed Moon, hurriedly pacing back and forth. They were at their usual place, in Clover Cricket Central, Twylar was most grateful school had been cancelled, as she could not stand another day of bullying. They decided to hang out in Sunset café. Moon closed it so they could have a bit of privacy.

Suddenly, a note hung in mid-air outside the window. Twylar could tell it was from the royal castle, as she had seen that stamp before. Suddenly, the window opened, and the letter opened by itself. See, magic was quite usual in the Circle of Kingdoms-oh, you don't know what the Circle of

Kingdoms is? Pay attention to your geography classes. But I will explain anyway, The Isle Of Irene, Dragon Thorn, Cosmic City, Volcano Hills, Bunny Town and Evergreen all make up the circle of kingdoms. Except Evergreen is more like a gateway into the circle rather than being a part of it. See, Evergreen isn't actually a kingdom; it's a city. Part of the real world. The Isle Of Irene is in the middle of the circle and is the biggest kingdom. All the other kingdoms make up the circle, with Evergreen being the gate out. However, there is one part of the circle which isn't a kingdom. 'The spirit forest,' they call it. It's filled with angry spirits, and anyone who goes in never comes out.

Well, as I was saying, magic was quite usual in the circle of kingdoms, but only royalty had the power. Everyone else living in the kingdoms was normal, Twylar, even though having royal blood, did not have any magic blood inside her. That was another strange thing about her. The letter read: Dear Twylar Irene, meet me at Moon Rose Avenue, 148. P. S. Come alone can bring company if desired as it would not matter. But coming alone would be preferable. Twylar's eyes widened in shock. Her friends stared worriedly at her. "Surely Stacey wouldn't snitch? Christie told her not to and she listens to her..." Lily whispered. "Well, you're not allowed to go out by yourself anyway, so I have to come." Sighed Ava.

Twylar snuck past the other guards stationed at the castle gates and slowly but surely made their way to Moon Rose Avenue. "Now we need to find house 148." Whispered Ava to Twylar. "Twy, if anything happens, I'll be outside the door." Pointing towards a dodgy-looking house. "Right, see ya!" agreed Twy, as she quietly tip-toed towards number 148 and knocked on the door. The door creaked open, and Ava stationed herself next to the window.

A person stood in front of Twylar menacingly. She could not see their face as it was covered by the person's hood. Suddenly, it spoke. "So you came?" Its voice was as sweet as sugar, and Twylar knew exactly who it was. "MUM!?" she squealed as her mother took off her hood. Revealing her luscious, wavy blonde hair. Her amber eyes stared into Twylar's. "Listen, I have something important to say, and you must not interrupt me." Twylar nodded and let her mother speak. "You know those ancient crystal wolves? Legend says they are all extinct. But that is wrong."

Twylar stared at her mother. "I am one of them. A werewolf, a crystal wolf." She continued. "There a seven types of crystal wolves, the Ruby wolf—the most wise; the Diamond wolf— the most honest; the Jade wolf—the most daring; the Amber wolf— the most cunning; the Gold wolf— the most kind. And, of course, the strongest of them all, the Amethyst wolf." She paused for breath.

She continued, "I'm a light amethyst wolf. The Amethysts are the only type of werewolves who have different species, such as the light amethyst, the dark amethyst, the dragon amethyst, and so on." Twylar let out an audible gasp whilst Ava, on the outside of the window, was trying to make sense of what was happening. "Well, I'm the last Amethyst, and I need to pass on my power to you before the crystal wolves actually go extinct. Look into my eyes, dear~" Amber's eyes were not their usual colour. Instead, they were purple, with cat-like slits for pupils. Before Twylar fell to the ground, she could see her mother had two ears on the top of her head; they were white, but they blended in with her hair colour. She had a white tail, and her eyes were now the usual amber. Twylar's vision had become very blurry. Her head had full impact on the ground.

Ava rushed in, but Amber had vanished. "Where did Queen Amber go? She was here a second ago.." questioned Ava, as she texted 'the legends' to come to their location. They carried Twylar to Moon's apartment. She and her family live on top of Sunset café, so they carried Twylar up the stairs, and Mrs Evers took a look at her. "Poor thing," she whispered under her breath as she went to get her medical box. When Twylar woke up, she found herself in a room; the walls were salmon pink, and the carpet was yolk yellow. Moon came into the room and explained where she was.

Well, it was comforting to know that at least Moon's family didn't think she was a demon or something, but she wasn't sure about that with Ava's little brother, as she had seen him before. He had hidden behind Ava, asking her to protect him from the 'demon'. These words stabbed Twylar in the chest, and she walked sulkily back to the castle. Only to get more upset by Sammy, Stacey and Christie. As Twylar headed to the kitchen, she bumped into Moon's little sister, "hi!" exclaimed Twylar, bending over to be at her height.

"Are you sissy's friend?" the little girl asked, Twylar nodded. "Oh! Twy, there you are, this is my little sis, Luna!" Moon Ran towards Twylar and hugged Luna. "People think I'm a demon too." Luna lifted up her leggings to reveal a very hairy leg. "I have something called 'monkey disease.' It makes some parts of your body very hairy." She sulked. "Well, I understand what you're feeling, but I get the most of it, being the king's daughter..." shouted Twylar as Luna disappeared into her room and slammed the door shut.

As Twylar sat down at the breakfast table, Mrs Evers had given both her and Luna two portions of sausage. Mr and Mrs Evers both had the same brown hair, which everyone in the family did, but dying your hair seemed to be a thing in the Evers family. Mrs Evers had dyed half her hair white, she was skinny and tall, she had green eyes, and her smile warmed up everyone's hearts. Mr Evers had not dyed his hair, but he had freckles and olive eyes, which sparkled with care. His hair was quite long, so long that every day, he had to tie it into a tiny ponytail. Moon was the eldest, so she was allowed to dye her hair pink at the bottom, but all her siblings were not allowed as they were too 'young' in Mrs Ever's eyes.

But, as Twylar began to eat, she could not stop thinking about what her mother had said at house 148, Moon Rose Avenue. The Legends met up again at Clover Cricket Central, and Twylar broke the news to them. "let's talk somewhere more private, like my house?" suggested Lily. Everyone groaned, but they knew she was right. As they braved the thorns and the darkness of the forest surrounding Lily's cottage, there was a letter wedged in her mailbox. Lily read it out loud. Twylar found out that Ava had been gifted a sword which could cut through anything, and its blade was made of hardened lava, no one except her could use it. Moon could summon massive meteors from up above, and control animals by will. Lily could transform into a giant siren, and Twylar was a dark amethyst.

All of that information was inside the ominous letter Lily was reading. Puzzled, Twylar stomped her foot in confusion. But everything went quiet. Everything was quiet and still. Her friends stopped moving. Twylar, realising from all the research she had done on amethyst wolves, had realised that being a dark amethyst meant she had powers. The dark amethyst was the most powerful type of amethyst wolf. She was kind of overwhelmed by that fact but shook it off. She was now wondering if she could control time. "Yes, you do," said the voice lazily. "Wha—?" Twylar spun her head round. "For the last time, no one's there," the voice drawled. "Well, yeah, you do have the power of time. Now go ahead and will for time to be unpaused— it's awfully quiet." Twylar stood still for a few seconds, then she willed with all her might for time to be unpaused, and it worked!

Twylar was relieved to see her friends blink, but they blinked quite a few times. "Am I hallucinating, or are you an actual crystal wolf?" wondered Moon in disbelief. Lily pointed wearily towards Twylar's big, black, feathery wings. Twylar's normal human ears had completely vanished. Twylar felt sick as she felt for her ears on the side of her head. Nothing was there. Instead, her ears were on top of her head. She had black ears, matching the hair on the back of her head. His great black tail had a white tip on the end of it. Twylar took one look at her wings and saw that there were white crystal-shaped things on the black feathers. It was on her tail and ears, too. "Let's go to Lion Rock Beach to test out our powers!" exclaimed Moon excitedly. "If Twy is a dark amethyst, then maybe the letter wasn't lying! And plus, it's autumn. No one will be there!"

Everyone agreed, and they set off for Lion Rock Beach. Twylar didn't know how to get rid of her ears and tail, so she hid them with her hood and shoved her tail up her t-shirt (which looked weird from the back) as they arrived. Moon's theory was proven correct. No one was there, Lily decided to test out her power first, so she ran up to the sea, since the letter said she was a giant siren, it was common knowledge that sirens are found in the water.

Lily jumped in, it had been a few minutes and the group of friends were starting to worry. They peered down at the calm, blue water in hopes of a speck of Lily's hair or one of the bracelets she wore on her wrist. But instead, they sprinted away as the water came crashing upon them. Lily had emerged from the water, but she didn't look like Lily anymore. Her usual, frizzy, dark brown hair was on top of her head, but now she had rough, green scales on her skin. Her face was not to be spared. All her makeup had been washed away by the water.

Her green scales were everywhere on her face, but she was still beautiful. (Except not really, in human form, she would.) She roared and looked around. In Twylar's eyes, she saw a colossal human being who had just turned into a siren. She shivered. The cold was getting at her now. Everyone wore shocked facial expressions. Lily took no notice but clasped her hand over her mouth. "I can't sing. When a siren sings, they can kill people," whispered Lily. But due to her size, they were able to hear her whisper quite clearly. She sunk into the water again and remerged as Lily. This time, she was not a siren. "I feel weird.." Lily touched around her face for any sign of scales. Everyone stared. It was soon Ava's turn, and she held out her hand mindlessly, for she hoped an invisible sword would be there. But as soon as she willed it to happen, a sword did appear. She grabbed it and sliced through a rock with ease. Moon wet everyone because of the giant splash she made (caused when she summoned meteors into the ocean), and a bird did come to her when she tested out her 'animal controlling' ability. Now, it was Twylar's turn.

She stood in front of everyone and pulled off her hood. Revealing her ears. She felt for her normal human ears but again felt sick at feeling patched-up skin where the ear should've been. She took a deep breath and willed with all her might to pause time, anything, but when she opened her eyes again, she was shorter than she had been before. She held her hands in front of her, but they were not hands. They were paws! She was a werewolf, and her fur was black, but little diamond shapes were all over her fur, white but the gem on her forehead seemed to be a glowing purple. Her wings were still black but she could see the rim and outline of it being white. There were gems on it, too, big, purple gems. Twylar stretched out her wings. She tried to talk, but all that came out of her mouth was just a bunch of woofing and barks. She willed to be human, and, ta-da! She was. But she no longer had her tail or ears, she felt anxiously for her human ears and was relieved to find they were there.

Chapter Three

After they all stopped complimenting and yapping on about each other's powers, they returned to their homes- or, in Twylar's case, tower. Twylar woke up more tired than she had been last night, but, the room was dark. She wasn't sure if she was in her room at all. Everywhere she turned was just black nothingness. She stared ahead and could see a beautiful woman who had long, silky black hair. She turned around and waved at Twylar. She had serpent-green eyes. Twylar recognised her immediately, but she didn't know who it was. She remembered her face... the hair... she turned around to see a man, a man with white hair, he had icy blue eyes.

He looked a lot like King William, but the glare in his eyes was what made William almost human. He glared not at Twylar but at the strange lady in front of Twylar. Suddenly, they attacked. They clashed together with what seemed like swords, but Twylar wasn't sure what it was, as they were holding ghostly silhouettes of what seemed like a sword. Twylar saw the isle Of Irene. It was up in flames, the strange lady screamed, and her skin started to harden...Twylar awoke. "Must've been a nightmare..." she thought, quickly dismissing the nasty thought in her head that was making her believe it was real.

She got ready, but as she was getting into her comfy clothes, a message from her dad floated through the hole in the roof. It opened itself and allowed Twylar to read it before tearing itself up. "OH BRUH!!" Twylar immediately flopped onto her bed, which was the worst decision ever, as her head slammed hard into the metal railings. Clutching her head tightly, she got changed into her normal uniform. As she began to climb down, she realised she could use her powers to fly down! "Don't you think people will get suspicious?" Twylar resented this voice. It somehow always weaselled its way into every part of Twylar's life. "And don't you think people will get sus if you suddenly started invading everyone's mind?" The voice paused for a second, "touché." It said sadly. "I'm tired of calling you the voice; what's your actual name!?" demanded Twylar, mid-climb. "Uhm, just call me Bella?" answered the voice. "Ok, hello, Bella, please find someone else's mind to invade," snapped Twylar.

A few minutes later, Twylar was repeatedly cleaning Christie and Stacey's room due to them purposely messing it up. After a hard day of work, Twylar managed to find some spare time to go out with The Legends. "Oh my gosh......" sighed Twylar. She shifted uncomfortably in her seat. The legends were taking a train to West Rose Moors, a small town near Rosaville. Everyone was staring at her. She moved closer to Lily, who was sitting next to her. She gave Twylar a reassuring smile. Finally, the dreaded train ride was over, and they got off at their destination. Twylar looked around. She had never been near West Rose Moors, but everyone seemed to know her.

Wherever she went, she could not escape it. Twylar hid herself behind Lily's back, and pulled her hood on so it engulfed her face completely. Soon, they had made it to Ava's parent's house. It was quite grand, except it was not a mansion, but it sure did look like one! The pointed roof was made of what seemed like pure silver, and the windows reflected the sky. Ava knocked on the door. It was the butler, Jaime, who opened it. "Howdy!" he waved cheerfully. But took one glance at Twylar and quickly looked away. He snorted in disgust. Ava sneered at him with a look so lethal it could kill an elephant. She climbed the stairs and took a left turn, gesturing for her friends to do the same. "I'd rather not." muttered Twylar, taking a step back. "Come on! My old mum can't do anything whilst she's sick, can she?" laughed Ava. "What about your brother?" Twylar caught a glimpse of a young boy with pale skin and jet-black hair. He shivered and ran upstairs, hiding from Twylar.

Soon, Twylar gave in and reluctantly allowed herself to be dragged up to the stairs, bumping on the velvet carpet. But, the voice had come back. "CUT DOWN THE TREE I HAVE WAITED TOO LONG!!!" it screamed. "Bella? DO YOU MIND SHUTTING UP!?" Twylar smacked her head hard, and found herself massaging it because of the pain. "NO! I WILL NOT! CUT IT DOWN!!!" Twylar's vision had become blurry—all she could see were squares and circles. She closed her eyes. For what seemed like hours, Twylar did not wake up. Instead, she was having the most curious dream. But it felt so real like she was watching real history right before her eyes. The strange thing is, it was just a tree. The same tree that lives in the middle of the castle is guarded day and night and protected by bulletproof glass. How coincidental!

Twylar managed to get through the day, and as she walked back to the castle, she saw a stooped figure of someone entering a suspicious black car. Twylar paused time and entered too; she un-paused time and waited for the car to stop. When it did, Twylar paused time AGAIN so she could get out without being seen. But, just as she touched the handle of the car, right there in front of her eyes, like a cinema, was everything to when the handle was made, to how many people had been using it, up until this very moment. Twylar thought about her newfound power. "Ok... time and Past? Yeah, I'll just call it that." Wondered Twylar. She willed herself out of the cinema sort of zone she was in, unpaused time and followed the figure into a strange blue warehouse. The paint peeled off the walls, and the walls had some rust on it. Twylar followed the man inside, only to her horror, she saw the figure take off its hood, revealing its white hair. "Dad?" thought Twylar. She paused time and took a closer look. Queen Amber was tied up; she was not wearing her crown, but on top of her head were a pair of white wolf ears, her tail in between her legs. She had a worried expression on her face. It looked as though she had recently been tortured. Twylar hid herself.

She unpaused the time. This power had proved itself useful up until now. King William shrieked with disgust. "To think my own wife was a werewolf... a crystal wolf!" he snorted. "I'm soon going to make crystal wolves extinct; they deserve to die! Filthy dogs." He sneered. He grabbed an axe from his servant and did the unthinkable. He killed his own wife. Twylar looked away. She did not care, though, as she knew that her time powers would be handy. If she could pause time, she could also rewind it!

But no matter how hard she willed it to happen, she couldn't. Now, it was time for her to panic. She sobbed quietly and stormed out. She transformed into a wolf and, using her impressive black wings, took flight and flew away as far as possible, away from the warehouse. With tears flooding her eyes, she waited at Lion Rock beach, knowing her friends would come. When they did come, they found a great black wolf quietly sobbing into its fur. The wolf transformed into Twylar in her werewolf form. Her ears on top of her head and tail hung low. She sobbed into Ava's arms, explaining in full detail the horrible thing she had witnessed. "I think we all have PTSD now..." shivered Moon as Twylar finished her story. Suddenly, Twylar could hear the same voice that had been invading her mind for the past four weeks. "I know what happened with Queen Amber", its voice shaking as if it had been crying. "You need to use your new powers on her dead body. NOW!" it screamed.

Twylar understood what she must do. Without a second thought, she transformed into a wolf, the little white crystals on her fur glistening. She spread her massive wings and took flight. She looked back and saw that Lily had transformed into a massive siren, except this time she had legs. She carried Ava, and with one step, she was already ahead of twylar. Moon was hanging upside down; she had summoned a small bird to carry her, but the bird was strong, it clutched onto Moon's clothes and carried her all the way to the blue warehouse. When they arrived, they saw that the black car Twylar had described had gone. Meaning they had killed Queen Amber, Twylar's mother.

Twylar was the first to burst through the doors (once she had transformed back into a human, in the case of werewolf hunters), and she jumped back in surprise. There, on the wooden pole in the middle of the warehouse, was Queen Amber. Her throat had been cut open, and her stomach was pierced. Twylar felt sick but bent over to her dead mother. She carefully placed her hand on Queen Amber's forehead and immediately saw her mother's whole life before her eyes. She skipped to the bit before she was tortured, and what she found out shook her to the bone. "William, dear! You don't want to do this! She is innocent, my dear! INNOCENT!!!" screamed Amber, her blonde hair all over the place. "Shut up, woman." Sneered the king's servant. "No, Camilla is not innocent! And she never will be! She almost destroyed the circle of kingdoms! Starting with our kingdom first!!!" shrieked King William. "You've gone mad... before you were the most beloved woman in the kingdom! You even stood up for that... demon." Snorted the servant. Twylar knew he was referring to her.

"Just you see! Someone will cut down the tree and set her free! Then you'll regret everything you've ever done! And here I am asking myself why I ever married such a foul, selfish, mental psychopath?" Queen Amber struggled to get out of the ropes that bound her, but she could not escape. "Enough! Harold, just for about... 20 minutes." And with that, the king walked out of the warehouse. Twylar saw 'Harold' lift an axe... she could not bear to watch.

She came back to reality—and snap!—everything fell into place. How could she not have realised it before, the strange voice that had been telling her to cut the tree down, those weird dreams? Twylar realised the seriousness of her situation. Now, with her mother gone, who was to protect her from being her dad's next victim? How would the Isle Of Irene react to her sudden death? Would they realise it was a murder?

Twylar decided to just sleep it off, as it had been nearing sunset. With a heavy heart, she trudged off towards the castle. Her limbs aching from climbing the roof to reach her tower, she flopped onto her bed. She took out her purple diary, the present her mother had gifted her. Tomorrow was Twylar's 16th birthday, and she was going to celebrate it with The Legends and not her mother. She eased her mind off anything that happened that day and fell into a deep sleep.

Twylar woke up to see a beautiful black-haired woman. With serpent green eyes... it was Camilla! Twylar reached out a hand for her great-aunt, but she saw the Isle of Irene in flames again. Was this the same dream? But as Twylar thought hard about what was going on, she suddenly found herself moving towards the castle. She climbed the stairs to reach the forbidden floor. She saw before her the tree that had been guarded day and night; the glass cover was smashed, the tree's usual blue leaves had turned brown, and the tree had been cut down.

Twylar awoke, but not to the birds chirping in the distance, but to the screams and shouts of people. She transformed into a wolf and flew out of the hole in the roof. When she was near ground level, she could see that everything was up in flames. Twylar hurriedly searched for any sign of her friends and was relieved to see that Ava, Moon and Lily were still alive. She flew down and told them all about her dream. "We're so dumb! How could we have not known!" exclaimed Ava, with a forced smile. "Camilla's innocent! Remember what Queen Amber said before she was tortured? Camilla was framed! And now she's trapped inside that stone statue of her in the middle of Clover Lily Central, and SHE'S THAT VOICE IN YOUR HEAD!!" Ava pointed at Twylar's forehead.

"If we cut down that blue tree, she'll be freed!" explained Ava. Suddenly, Mrs Evers hurriedly approached them. "What are you girls doing here? You need to evacuate now!" she shrieked. But Twylar ran in the opposite direction, towards the castle. When she entered, she saw her dad standing in front of her. "I know you were watching me kill that... wolf woman." He said darkly. "I'm going to put an end to your miserable life! You demon!" he shrieked. See, as he was royalty, he had special abilities, I'm sure I explained this to you in some part of the story, but only royals have special skills or powers. Up until the day Twylar met her mother at Moon Rose, she had been powerless. Which was strange as she was of royal blood.

The king cackled and huge portals of darkness were on both sides of him. Out crawled monstrous beasts. They were like giants, except they had the skulls of moose and bodies of an ape. They carried with them giant metal clubs with spikes on them, and hurled them at Twylar. Whenever they threw their clubs, they always came flying back to their owner after they had hit their target. Twylar had no choice but to dodge. Much to her luck, she found that giant meteors had destroyed the ceiling. She knew that her friends were there. Moon summoned deadly snakes to bite the monsters, and they retreated to the portal.

"Guys!" exclaimed Twylar, looking around at her friends, who stood loyally behind her. "GET READY TO GET WRECKED, YOU OLD PIG!!!" shouted Ava as she charged with her sword. But the King smiled and disappeared into one of his portals. "Hurry, Ava! You need to cut down the tree with your sword! Then Camilla will be free!" yelled Twylar as she ran to the forbidden floor. "Moon! Use your meteors to destroy the glass!" moon nodded and destroyed the ceiling and the glass. "WAIT!! MY DIARY!" realised Twylar. "Go get it! I'll cut down the tree!" yelled Ava as she prepared to strike. The cursed blue. That was the name of the tree, anyway. Its leaves were blazing blue, a much brighter shade than Ava's hair. Its roots twisted in a knot deep beneath the grass, the glass dome which Moon had shattered lay in pieces across the marble floor. Twylar quickly transformed and flew into her tower. This would be the last time she ever saw it again. Making sure she had her diary tucked safely in her bag, she transformed into a werewolf, picked up the bag and flew out to Clover Lily Central to see if Ava had really cut down the tree. Sure enough, her friends were all there, and Camilla's statue was no longer there, too. "I'M FREE!!" she shrieked, jumping everywhere.

"Wait... ARE YOU BELLA!??" asked Twylar, realising that Camilla's voice seemed familiar. She was just as beautiful as she was in Twylar's dream, her long, straight, black hair flowing in the wind. She had a small fringe, and her green eyes glistened. She transformed into a black horse, "HOP ON, I'LL EXPLAIN LATER!!" she yelled. So, the Legends huddled onto Camilla's back (that sounds weird, bear with me), and they took off!

Once they were in the safety of the woods, Camilla explained who she was and what she was. "So, you're a wingless?" asked Moon blindly. "Yes, just like Twylar's a dark amethyst!" she exclaimed cheerfully. She dropped the twigs and sticks they had collected and started a fire. They cooked some fish that Moon had caught, and realising they were on the edge of the kingdom, they began to explore the forest more freely. "Guys,

Jerry's just given me the news." Announced Moon over breakfast. "Go on?" enquired Camilla. "The king's saying Twy set you free, blah blah and that you destroyed the kingdom with the help of his powers. He fixed the castle, and everyone truly believes you've gone down the same path as Camilla." She paused abruptly. "But Camilla's been framed so…" she continued with her breakfast. "Wait, who's Jerry?" asked Camilla. "Oh, just my pet robin. He's such a coward I don't know how he managed to fly to the castle and back!" Moon rolled her eyes. Jerry chirped angrily and started pecking at Moon's hair. As they continued their life in the forest, it was clear they were no longer safe in the forest.

Ava had sworn that she saw one of the royal guards patrolling the area. King William wanted to make sure they were gone for good. "Well, nowhere's safe now that we're refugees." Announced Ava. "So maybe we can search by air for the other refugees?" suggested Twylar. "Well, my family and probably a few other people are the only refugees, and by other people, I mean Lindy." Groaned Moon. Lindy was a nickname for Linda, but to be honest, she was a brat. The brattiest of brats in the entire world, actually not IN THE ENTIRE UNIVERSE!!

But, she wasn't as bad as Christie, Stacey and Sammy, but she was, let's put it like this. She's the daughter of a rich businessman from the real world, so she's an outsider to the circle of kingdoms. All she's ever known of life is just big, busy cities and the smell of petrol. Ever since she moved to the Isle of Irene, she's been cornering The Legends, and she pretends like she's a part of their friend group when she's not. So now, can you see why everyone hates her? Not just The Legends, it's everyone who's ever had the misfortune to meet her. Lindy's just generally a very nosy person. She even has a big nose to scream out loud, "I'M NOSY. I WANNA SEE WHAT Y'ALL ARE DOING!!" But, while the group was searching the forest, they found Moon's family, Lindy (Moon let out an audible groan) and Willow. "WILLOW!!!" Twylar shrieked as she hugged her best friend. "What are you doing back here? I thought you moved to Evergreen?" wondered Lily as she too, came in for a hug. "Ha-ha I guess I moved back at the wrong time?" she shrugged. "Someone needs to back me up on all the drama!" she exclaimed as she sat down on one of the logs.

After explaining, they headed straight for bed. None of them had brought sleeping bags, so they each made a pillow made out of leaves and just learned to cope with the cold as they didn't have a duvet. Of course, Lindy tried her best to involve herself in group chats with The

Legends, but Moon was having none of it. "Linda, you're not our friend, and you never will be. Go make yourself useful before I make you our dinner!" roared Moon angrily. Trust me, you don't want to be around Moon while she's angry. Linda sulked and ran away, trying her best to do a 'cute bubbly girl' cry, which sounded more like a cry from an eagle.

"Shut up, barbie" whispered Twylar. She hated Linda, but at least she was not as mean as Twylar's sisters and Sammy. She was just plain annoying. The next day, Willow realised something important. "Guys, we're being watched. She whispered hurriedly, but they had forgotten. Today was the day the refugees were supposed to travel to another kingdom they had been separated. And the worst part is Linda was still there. Willow stared uncomfortably at a random bush. Suddenly, creatures with black cloaks and hoods surrounded them. They knocked them all out cold. Twylar woke up in what seemed like a fancy hotel room, but everything was purple. She looked outside and realised they weren't on The Isle of Irene anymore. They were in Cosmic City. It's well known for its crazy prince and psycho king, and Autumn is the month they hold the most popular tournament of all…

A guard knocked on Twylar's door. It opened. "The king has ordered you to come to the great hall now!" he said roughly as he dragged Twylar out. Once she arrived, she stared at the throne. Beside it, were her friends, Camilla and Lindy. Well, Twylar wasn't at all bothered about Lindy. "You will participate in the Death Trials, a monthly event held by Cosmic City. My son, the Cosmo prince, will be watching this event as well as our civilians! If you lose, you will die, and your friends here will rot in our dungeons!" a figure emerged from the shadows. "Guards, take her to the first trial. The trial of the Black Dragon!" a boy followed the guards. He had freckles and dark purple hair, and he was wearing a black jester suit, which had dark purple stripes on it. He quickly put on a creepy-looking mask; it had a picture of a moon with a face on it.

Twylar was led to a stone room. There was a window on the other side, and Twy's friends were on the outside, along with The Cosmo Prince and The King. "Welcome to the trial of the Black Dragon. You will have to find a key whilst blindfolded and whilst that stone dragon down there is slowly filling your room with boiling lava!" laughed the prince. He pointed to a dragon below Twylar, and as they spoke, it was filling the room with lava. Twylar put on her blindfold. She realised the Cosmo

Prince didn't say she couldn't use powers, so she transformed into a werewolf and sniffed out the key.

"Well, it can't be that easy, right?" snorted the king. He pressed a red button, and the lava was rising faster than before. She hurriedly searched the air mindlessly for the key before feeling cold metal. She grabbed it, and the lava, which was nearing her feet, slowly disappeared. She took off her blindfold to see the relieved faces of her friends. She wiped some sweat from her eyebrows before being led to the second trial. "The trial of the monkey king. Climb this mountain and rescue his sire's pet rock." Announced a guard, referring to the Cosmo Prince. He took off his mask, and his curly, purple hair waved in the wind. He gave Twylar a look which said, "Do your best!" she smiled. Realising again that no one had mentioned the use of powers, she transformed into a wolf and ran up the steep mountain walls.

She decided she could just fly up, so she did. Once she reached the top, she transformed into a werewolf, her tail wagging at the thought of her finally getting to leave this horrid place. She was surrounded by monkeys, and without thinking, she opened up a portal with dark chains that dragged the monkeys into them.

"Woah! A new power!" thought Twylar excitedly. She tried to focus so she could pause time but was distracted by the huge golden doors opening. There was a gold building at the top of the mountain, and she stepped back. Out came a massive monkey. "This is probably the monkey king.." she wondered. She prepared to fight, but the massive ape sent her flying, and she tumbled down to Earth. She hid in a corner and held back her tears. She did not want to lose her friends and only living relatives just when her mother had died! As she cried, her tail turned white, her ears too.

Instead of the crystals on her fur being white, they were yolk-yellow. She grabbed a broken bit of glass, which was shiny enough to reflect her face. Instead of the normal black burn patch and black eyes, Twylar's burn patch had become yellow, her left eye's iris (which was usually black) had turned yellow, and her cat-like pupil remained white. Her hair, now a very light blonde, looked nothing like it had before. Her rear hair, which was usually white, was now yellow. She looked at the bruises and cuts she'd received from the fall. It was all healed! Twylar paused time, but as she did so, her tail and ears were black again, and her burn patch and left eye were black. With a lot of unanswered questions in her mind, she forced herself to break inside the building and rescue The Cosmo prince's pet rock.

As she crept out, the Monkey King noticed her and rampaged. He charged at Twylar, who dived out of the way, she had no choice but to quickly transform and jump. She used her massive black wings to make sure she didn't turn into human jelly when she neared the ground. Everyone was shocked to see Twylar had returned. The trial of the Monkey King was supposed to be the trial that finished her off! Angered, the king sped off towards his castle. The Cosmo Prince gave her a relieved look before running off to his dad. Twylar was still confused about what happened up the mountain, so she went to search for the Cosmo Prince.

Once she finally found him, she panted. "Why are you here?" he asked, turning around. "Well, up on the mountain, I was badly injured, but suddenly my tail, wings and ears turned white, my black burn patch turned yellow, and my black eye too!" she explained, pointing to her burn patch. "Well, you're a dark amethyst, right? Your mother is a light amethyst?" he inquired. "Yeah..?" questioned Twylar. "Well, my guess is that you inherited a bit of your mother's species of Crystal wolf, so when your fur turned white, you became a light amethyst like your mother." He guessed. "Oh! Thanks, Cosmo prince?" she exclaimed. "My name's actually Alexander, but call me Alex!" he smiled. Tomorrow would be the final trial. She had to rest. She needed it for the big day. As she sunk into her bed back in the hotel room, she could hear a door creaking open. "That's her, sir." Said a gruff voice. "Thank you, Wilbert; make sure the next trial kills this demon and her freaky friends." Said another voice. Twylar recognised it as her dad's voice. "What's my dad doing here?" wondered Twylar.

Just then, someone else came through the open door. "Wake up!!" it hissed. Twylar immediately recognised this voice as Alex opened her eyes. "You need to escape! The next trial is basically your dad trying to kill you!!!" he exclaimed. "Yeah, I know.. what about my friends?" she asked. "I set them free; they're waiting for you at the gate!" he explained. Once Twylar had reached the gate, Twylar saw her friends' worried faces. Alex came along, too, and everyone stared at him. "What? I can't stay with my crazy dad forever, can I?" he asked. Twylar transformed into a wolf and took flight. Camilla was right beside her. Moon and Ava were riding on the backs of horses, and Willow was riding on a cloud.

(another ominous letter came their way and said that Willow could control the weather.)

And, of course, being royalty, Alex had his own powers, but they were no good for travelling. So he, too, rode on the back of a horse. They reached the bridge that connected The Isle Of Irene with Cosmic City, which took about a whole day. Dawn was breaking, and they reached the tangled forests of The Isle Of Irene. They settled down near a river and caught fish for their brunch. "I wonder if the king's burned down sunset café.." groaned Moon. "Wait, where's Linda?" realised Ava, looking around. "I hope she was forgotten and Alex didn't set her free!" said Twylar cheerily. "What? That blonde girl?" asked Alex. "Yeah, I did set her free, but she wasn't at the gate", everyone groaned. Alex pointed at the river, and Linda emerged from the water. Her clothes were ripped, and her hair was like heaven for headlice, "hello my dear friends! It is I, the great Lind- AAAA" she screamed as lightning struck her. "My bad," said Willow cheekily. She was a hero to everyone there. Alex, who then realised that Linda was a brat, started cheering.

Twylar felt a little bad and helped Linda back up. She cleaned her up and gave her some spare clothes she'd 'borrowed' from the hotel room. That night, Alex unpacked his awfully big bag and pulled out some tents. They set them up, but they had to share as there were only 3. Ava slept with Willow and Twylar, Moon slept with Camilla, and Alex had one to himself. Linda was forced to sleep outside, but she had said the next day that she quite liked sleeping on a tree. The next day, Alex had become a part of 'The Legends' and they set off for Bunny Town. They needed their army if they wanted to defeat the King!

Even though Bunny Town is inhabited only by cute, adorable bunnies, their army has no mercy. They will trick you with their cuteness and when you reach out a hand to pet them, they will bite it off. WITH NO MERCY! As soon as they had reached the gates, they got off the black car driven by Willow, and followed her inside the castle. Normally, people would scream in disgust and fear as soon as Twylar entered a room, but the bunny inhabitants shrugged. Twylar felt safe for once in her life. She felt loved. Sure, she had her friends back then, but still, they could not protect her from all the gloom and sorrow in her life. It's so comforting that, for once in her life, no one pointed at her burn patch or ran away as she stared them down with her peculiar eyes. She could get used to Bunny Town!

The Legends were now in the courtroom, bowing before the Bunny King. "You want my army, hmm?" questioned the king as he beckoned for his daughter to come. "This is Estella, my daughter. you are staying here for two weeks, probably enough to make up my decision." He said irritably, and Estella was not a bunny. She was a human, probably the only human here! "Well, guys, I gotta go back to Linda; you still have your phones?" Willow pulled out her pink phone, which had a cute cat charm on it and what seemed like a friendship heart, which all the girls had. "How come I don't have one of those?" Alex pointed to the heart charm on Willow's phone.

"Oh, it's a best friend thing, we did it before you were in the group!" answered Twylar cheerily. Estella waved and skipped over to them. She had long, curly, light pink hair which was up to her waist, she was wearing a black and white striped t-shirt and had an also pink cardigan on top. "Hello! Twylar Irene, isn't it? I've heard so much about you!" she hugged Twylar, who immediately knew she had become a part of The Legends. Estella hugged everyone (except for Willow as she had gone back to Camilla and Linda) before finally landing on Alex. He had been so quiet it seemed as if he was dead when Estella greeted him all he did was just bluntly shake her hand. They all got separate rooms. The next day, Willow joined them and The Legends weren't separated any more. Twylar told her all about yesterday and how weird Alex had acted around Estella. Ava had bonded with the commander of the bunny army; he was quite impressed when she showed him her power and how only she could use it. Moon had discovered Estella also had a love for baking, but her baked goods were a work in progress. Moon spent the entire day teaching her how to bake an apple pie without burning it!

Willow was busy practising her power outside, so there were sudden thunder strikes and then a gush of wind, or perhaps there would be a staircase made of clouds for Willow to climb. Alex was forced into telling Twylar what had made him so flustered when Estella tried to hug him. In the end, he gave up and told Twylar everything. "Listen, Twy, I kinda.. like Estella.." he murmured. Twylar's excitement bottled up inside her before she could not hold it any longer. She immediately began forming plans to ask her out, all to Alex's dismay. "I appreciate your help, but isn't that enough?" he cried as Twylar led him to Willow's room. Alex just curled himself up and covered his face. Most people say he's crazy, just like his dad, but he's honestly just super easily flustered and just a really timid guy. "No wonder he wears that creepy mask!" remarked Willow. Alex had some courage to take it off, thanks to The Legends' support, but now this conversation was making him want to put it on again.

Camilla and Linda were invited to stay at Bunny Town, and everyone was sworn not to tell Twylar's dad that she and Camilla were at Bunny Town. If they did, they'd have to face the bunny army AND Ava, who was mercilessly cruel in battle. Whilst Alex and Twylar had become the best of all friends, Estella had also gotten to know Twylar a little bit more. As she insisted that she and Twy should go on a walk to explore the city, Twylar was filled with the constant reminder of what her father had done. The image of her mother being brutally killed remained embedded in her mind forever. But she thought back to what had happened in Cosmic City. She had transformed into a Light Amethyst. She had inherited her mother's species and the dark amethyst. Twylar smiled.

She finally changed into the new clothes that Estella had given her. She was glad to be out in the fresh air! As Estella showed Twylar around the kingdom, it seemed as if she could tell what Twy was thinking. "I know you want to know why I'm the only human here. Everyone does!" she said with a faded smile. Twylar shifted uncomfortably on the hard, wooden bench they were huddled upon. "Well, I'm not actually from the circle of kingdoms. I'm an outsider, a foreigner," she began, "but.. my real parents never cared for me. They like my brother more."

"And.. what was his name?" Twylar was urging her on silently.

"His name was Jaime. He was a terrible big brother" the mood had changed very suddenly. She hung her head low. "Well, he used to hit me and blame me for things he did." She whimpered, "My parents eventually didn't want me and left me like garbage here in Bunny Town." Twylar put her hand on Estella's shoulder and smiled reassuringly.

"The king found me as I was quite easy to spot. Being the only human here!" she laughed. "He realised what situation I was in and banished my parents from ever coming here again." Twylar knew how that felt all her life; she had been thought to be a 'scary demon' and her father, Stacey, Christie, Sammy.

"What were they all doing now?" thought Twylar. "So, he adopted me.. and now I'm a foreign princess of a kingdom full of non-humans." Her voice shook a bit.

"I.. understand what you're feeling."

Estella raised her eyebrow. "all my life… My dad, My own siblings and their friends…" Twylar sulked

"They've been bullying me my whole life.. everyone thinks I'm a demon, my mum was murdered by my dad, I DON'T KNOW WHAT TO DO ANYMORE!!" she shrieked. She clasped her hands to her face and cried. She cried for her dead mother, she cried for the way she had been treated her whole life, and she cried because she could not believe in the span of about 4 weeks all this had happened. The fire, Camilla's escape, Bella actually being Camilla (you know, that voice in Twylar's head?), she could not believe how quickly chaos had struck. Surprisingly, the news that Twylar and The Legends had reached Bunny Town didn't actually spread to the king, so that's lucky! Moon used her 'animal-controlling' power to convince a bird to fly over to her family, bearing a note in its tiny claws. All the refugees came from different kingdoms; Moon's family and Willow's mum came from the dark forests of The Isle Of Irene, and practically everyone forgot about the dangerous situation they were in. Alex finally convinced Willow and Twylar to stop annoying him by making up random love stories about him and Estella, so now he just stares at her wishing he had the courage to go up to her and talk. Mrs Evers had opened up 'Bunny Bakery', the bunny-suitable version of Sunset café. Moon had offered Estella a position there, to which she gladly agreed. Soon, Bunny Bakery was drowned by a flock of hungry bunnies. They munched happily on their carrot cakes and carrot stew, with carrot juice on the side. "They sure do like carrots.." yawned Moon as she emptied out the trash for the 8th time. "Yeah.." replied Estella, half-asleep with her head on the counter. Since there wasn't enough room for Moon's family to live in the castle, they lived on top of Bunny Bakery, which, convenient enough, looked exactly like their apartment back at The Isle Of Irene!

Life seemed happy, and best of all, no one gave Twylar weird looks as she passed by or had a royal guard follow her everywhere. She stared absent-mindedly at a bush. She made her way slowly back towards the mighty bunny castle. She took a look at one of the gruesome bunny guards. "They don't look friendly at all…" wondered Twylar. As she was walking, with her head fixed on the bunny guard, she banged her head into the wall. It was throbbing with pain, and she touched it gently. Without a second thought, she had transformed into a Light Amethyst and healed herself. The pain had evaporated, leaving Twylar relieved the pain in her head was dying down. Immediately before her, the ghostly white outline of.. someone?

"Ah! My dear, I see you have inherited my species of Amethyst, the Light Amethyst!" it said. It walked over to Twylar, held her tight, and suddenly, she was spinning around at rapid speed. "Almost there!" screamed the ghost of Amber. Twylar held on to her dead mother for her life. This is weird because normally, you can go through ghosts, but Twylar could feel her mother's clothes very clearly. It was the clothes she had worn before she was murdered.

"How.. how are you here?" stuttered Twylar as the spinning stopped. She found herself in what seemed like a white box, but she was sure it was just white nothingness. She stretched her arm out nervously. Nothing happened. "Well, remember that night? At Moon Rose? When I transferred my powers to you?" asked Amber...Twylar turned around and stared at her dead mum's soulless eyes. She still had her beauty, her blonde hair drooping over her shoulders, her amber eyes staring into Twylar's. "Yeah..?" remembered Twylar attentively. Her focus is entirely on the ghostly figure before her. "When I gave you my power, I gave you a part of my soul, too. Wherever you are, I won't be far to follow!" she smiled and led Twylar into the white nothingness. Suddenly, before her, she saw Camilla fighting with William (Not her dad, the one that imprisoned Camilla in her statue.) "What's this supposed to mean?" murmured Twylar to herself. She was led to another place in time. This time, William had Camilla in chains. The tree that Ava had cut back in The Isle Of Irene was there, its blue leaves swaying gently. William plucked one of the leaves and force-fed it to Camilla. Her body started to harden, and she soon became the statue she was imprisoned with for over a decade!

Queen Amber led Twylar away, and soon, they both began to spin again. Twylar found herself outside the gates of the bunny castle, The Legends were looking at her with a worried expression. It was Ava who carried Twylar to the hospital wing. The bunny nurse took one look at her and declared she was fine. Immediately after, The Legends had made themselves snug in Lily's room, and Twylar told them the whole story. "So now we know how Camilla was turned to stone, I guess," murmured

Moon as she drank the rest of her hot chocolate. "Wait, where is Camilla?" asked Ava, looking around. "Don't worry, she's downstairs with Linda!" smiled Estella. Ava sighed with relief. "Uhm, why did Queen Amber show you that then? AND HOW IN THE WORLD DO YOU HAVE A BIT OF HER SOUL INSIDE YOU!!??" shrieked Alex as he slammed his mug on the table. "I don't know... WHY AM I THE ONE THAT HAS TO SUFFER!?" screamed Twylar as she slapped herself in the face. Immediately regretting it, she transformed into a Light Amethyst and healed herself. "Hmm, maybe, like with your Dark Amethyst form, you might have more than one power!" exclaimed Lily excitedly. Twylar concentrated, and suddenly, a rush of adrenaline came to her veins. She stared at her friends, then at her hands. Well, we say hands, but they were actually paws. Like with the Dark Amethyst wolf form, her fur in that form was all black, with little white gems all over her fur. Her burn mark remained on her wolfy face, her eyes the same, but in the Light Amethyst wolf form, Twylar's wings had turned light yellow, her fur white and the tiny gems yellow, her burn mark was light yellow, and her eyes had also been affected by this. She transformed back and smiled in amazement. "Well, technically, that's not a power, is it?" huffed Lily. Twylar tried to concentrate again. This time, the adrenaline seemed different. It corrupted her mind and controlled her body. Suddenly, Pale yellow fire shot out of her palms. She tried to stop, but in the end, they had to splash her hands with water. "Cool!!" exclaimed The Legends at once. They all rushed towards Twylar and talked non-stop about the yellow flames that had shot out her palms. She bid goodnight to her friends and shut the door of her room behind her. She lay in bed, thinking about the events of today. The white nothingness. Her mother. The yellow flames. She managed to rest for a few hours before waking up to the sound of her alarm clock. "Life in Bunny Town certainly is great!" thought Twylar as she put on her shoes. She looked out her window, and saw Willow was practising her powers. AGAIN. A dark thundercloud followed her everywhere she went. She seemed delighted that it had grown tenfold in size immediately after a battery was thrown at it. Moon dragged Estella across the floor, ready for another tiresome day of running Bunny Bakery. "You didn't tell me running a bakery would be this exhausting!" Estella whined. "Didn't think I needed to. Plus, I already have experience because of Sunset Café." Moon snorted. Ava was showing off her skills in swordsmanship to the chief commander of the bunny army, he clapped his hands -paws- in delight.

Twylar, who you would seem to feel left out as she watched all this, felt happy. She was glad everything was coming along so nicely! She couldn't stop thinking about what had happened yesterday, though. Is it true a fragment of Queen Amber's soul lives within Twylar? Well, probably what better explanation for what had happened yesterday? She tied her shoelaces, finishing with a neat bow. She ran outside to meet her great-grandmother, who was kept young by her stony prison. Twylar hugged Camilla, squeezing so tight that she couldn't breathe. "Woah, take it easy!" laughed Camilla as she gently pushed Twylar aside. She smiled. "ready for our walk then?" she asked. "Yeah!" agreed Twylar.

The two set off into the park. Everything whipped past. In a couple of weeks, autumn would be over. And winter's harsh, icy breath would gnaw at people's skin, and the trees would be caked in glittery snow. For now, even though the autumn breeze sliced against Twylar's skin, the calm, fiery leaves on the trees swayed, and the ground was littered with all sorts of things, like twigs and branches, and an avalanche of leaves were piled up. Bunny children were jumping into it, laughing and playing. Twylar smiled but shivered as the cold got to her. Camilla held her in her arms. With Queen Amber gone, Camilla was like a second mother to Twylar. She cherished this moment. Knowing it would never last too long. They sat down at a bench and watched the children play.

Suddenly, Camilla spoke. "Well... back in the good old days," she began. Twylar listened attentively. "I remember... everyone loved me. Back then, The Isle Of Irene was not a racist kingdom. They loved someone for who they are, not what they look like." She sighed. Twylar urged her on. "Remember when I was 'Bella', that voice in your head?" Twylar nodded her head. "I made you relive your very worst memories... and I'm really sorry for that. I was angry. Anger can make you do very horrible things!" she apologised. Twylar responded with yet another hug. She stared into Camilla's serpent-green eyes. Her waist-long, straight black hair hung in front of Twylar's face. She did not mind, though. She wanted this moment to last forever. No one could ever understand how it feels like to be somewhere where you are always loved, never judged, and understood. Back home, Twylar would be washing clothes, tidying the castle and dealing with Christie, Stacey and Sammy. She remembered her sisters' white hair. The thing she was supposed to have. But, being Camilla's descendant, she had inherited her black hair. Twylar got off the bench and walked to a small puddle. She looked at her reflection. Her rear hair was white, and the back of her head was black. Two-tone.

Just then, she remembered. It was an old memory. Twylar was still in primary school, around the age of nine or ten. That was when she met Willow. Even though Sammy, Christie and Stacey bullied her, she had her friends for support. Ava had her silky black hair tied in a ponytail, her white bow at the back. Moon's hair was short, her dark brown hair tied in pigtails. Lily was wearing a blue beanie on her head, her dark hair in braids. Willow was new to Woden Hills. She used to live in Evergreen. Of course, she did not know anything about Twylar, so the moment she saw her, she decided she needed a bit of love. She ran over and asked to be friends, much to Twylar's delight. The next day, in the playground, Willow, Ava, Moon and Lily formed a circle around Twylar. They chatted and played and had a good time. Until the troublesome trio came marching into the playground. The 'troublesome trio' is what the girls call Stacey, Christie and Sammy. They shoved and pushed, leaving Ava with a black eye. Twylar stood, cowering before the three great giants, but Willow was having none of it. I didn't fully explain to you how she looked. Right now, she has brown hair tied in space buns, she has brown skin and she did NOT give up without a fight.

Willow, even though she was smaller than Sammy, attempted to shove her back. However, a teacher did catch Willow and she had detention for a week! Twylar was made to clean Christie and Stacey's rooms, just for existing. It was at this moment that Twylar realised, Willow and all her friends were loyal. They fought for her, they encouraged her to stand up.. even against the tallest mountain this world has ever seen. She wiped a tear from her eyes, realising that there might be hope.. the thing that lights the way for Twylar as she struggles in the dark tunnel of her childhood. Twylar stared into the puddle as she remembered. There might be hope.

Camilla walked over to her and smiled. "I still have access to your memories. But it's fading away now, so I won't be able to access it after today." She whispered. Twylar hugged her, hugged her so tight that Camilla staggered back. The two then began the walk back to the castle. They held hands. Grandmother and granddaughter. Camilla smiled at Twylar as she headed off to her room. Feeling sleepy, she headed to her room only to find Alex sitting on her bed. "What're you doing here?" she hissed. "I'm tired I need to sleep!" Alex got off the bed and hurriedly explained why he was there. "Why are Willow and Estella after you!?" she laughed. "Could you keep it down?" he whispered, looking around nervously. "Uhm.. yeah, so I kinda promised Willow I would tell Estella that I like her, but then I promised Estella that I'd take her to see the fireworks and"- he began. "You broke them?" asked Twylar in the middle of his sentence. "Yes, and now, if you want me to live, please find a spot for me to hide!" he whispered hurriedly.

"Ok, fine, fine! Follow me. I know a place." Twylar whispered back. "Thanks, Twy!" feeling relieved, Alex followed Twylar deeper into the castle until they reached the castle library. "Hide here, and you are welcome, by the way." Snorted Twylar as she headed back to her room. "Thanks, Twy! You're a life-saver!" he half-shouted, half-whispered. She tip-toed back to her room and lay in bed, thinking if Alex was planning to sleep down there in the library or if Willow had found him and electrocuted him! With a lot of thoughts on her mind, she managed to push them aside, and she drifted off into a deep sleep. The next day, The Legends decided to practise their powers. Willow was practising her weather powers,

Moon summoned huge meteors that crashed onto the field, and Lily became a massive siren (in this form, she had scaly, green legs!) Estella was practising the powers she was naturally born with (probably another reason why her parents didn't like her much), and Alex had just found out that he could practically become Harry Potter and had made poor Ava float. When Ava had come down again, she continued to cut through harder and harder objects with her sword. She asked Moon to lift it and use it, but she couldn't. Only if Ava allowed her. Twylar was practising all of her powers. She became a dark amethyst and paused time, and as she un-paused it, she tapped a blade of grass, and before her, she could see it as a tiny seedling growing into the grass. Then, once she willed herself out of whatever zone she was in, she summoned a dark portal right in front of her, and out came from it black chains. They uprooted a nearby tree and pulled it into the dark abyss of the portal. After the portal evaporated from sight, Twylar transformed into a light amethyst and shot the pale yellow flames from out her hands. With a bit of control, she managed to stop the flames and moved on to her next power. Healing. She had no cuts or bruises to heal, so she made one. She punched hard metal with her fist and healed it using her powers.

She huffed and sighed and prepared herself for round two. She had been practising her powers like this for a while now. However, she couldn't stop herself from getting distracted. They had come to Bunny Town for their army; it's almost been two weeks, and the King hasn't made a decision! What if they don't get the army? How will they save the circle of kingdoms? With a billion thoughts racing through her mind, she had not realised Willow was gone. When The Legends became aware of her disappearance, they checked her room. And on her bed was a note. Lily picked it up and read it out loud. "It's me, Willow. You guys really thought I liked you? Hah! Think again! The King's got the one thing needed to defeat you, The Blossom of Life! Since you guys cut down that blue tree, we're planting a new one to imprison you and your freaky friends! All we need is spirit souls. Bye, losers! -Willow"

The silence was unbearable. "That means.. the king's gone to the spirit forest, and... Willow betrayed us..." said Alex shakily. "We have to stop them from getting those souls! Who's with me?" added Estella as she put her hand out. Twylar was the first to put her hand out. Soon followed by the rest. "Alright, that's settled. We're leaving for Spirit Forest as soon as we get the bunny army. Estella, try to convince your dad to make a decision soon. Time is short!" announced Ava as she crumpled up the letter and threw it with disgust. "Betrayer.." she whispered angrily as she sped out of the room. Alex looked at Twylar, and she looked back. The looks meant: "Ava's gone mental" Then, they hurried off to the dining room to eat their dinner.

The other day, Willow electrocuted Alex for breaking his promise, and in the end he did take Estella to see the fireworks. He almost mustered up the courage to tell her how he truly felt, but he couldn't. Lily and Twylar decided to go to the beach, but they made sure it wasn't one that was near The Isle Of Irene! Lily transformed into a massive siren once they reached their destination, and she ended up creating a tsunami that headed Twylar's way. "Oops.. sorry, Twy!" she giggled as Twylar emerged from the water, her hair and clothes drenched in cold water. While Lily and Twylar were having fun on the beach, Estella and Moon had closed Bunny Bakery, and the two (and Moon's family) went to a museum which held the history of how Bunny Town came to be. Alex and Ava were the only ones who were planning the attack on the king. Linda tried to join in, saying that she was 'much smarter and prettier than them in every way' In the end, Alex used his levitating powers on her, and she floated back to the castle. Camilla did join them a few hours later, then followed by the rest of The Legends after they had finished their day out. "Estella, has your dad made a decision yet?" asked Ava as she spread a map of the circle of kingdoms across the table. "Well, he said he's thinking about it!" said Estella, in her normal honey-sweet voice. "I think when we get the army, we should send some agents to The Isle Of Irene to see what Dad's planning." Added Twylar. Everyone agreed. "Sorry to break the mood, but my dad made an alliance with The

Isle Of Irene, so it would be a full-on war!" blurted out Alex. "Ok, one, what is with the dad's two? IT ALREADY IS A WAR!!" shouted Moon.

She stared at everyone and sighed, "It's like history's repeating itself. The thing that happened to Camilla might happen now." She huffed. Everyone turned their heads towards Camilla. "Well, yeah, the thing is, we have to stop the king from getting those souls." She sighed. Twylar took the lead and grabbed a pen from Lily. She began to draw lines, then shapes. Suddenly, in front of them, they saw what looked like a sunken cove deep beneath the sea. "When I was younger, my mum told me stories of an ancient myth. It was called 'The Drowned'." She began. Everyone fell silent. "Apparently, hidden deep in the oceans of Dragon Thorn lies a small cove. They called it The Drowned, hence the name of the myth. And it's home to Shavanii, the sea demon." She drew what seemed like a massive octopus, but the octopus had sharp teeth and teeth after that, all the way along the inside of its neck. She labelled it 'Shavanii' and turned to face her friends. "And it just so happens this sea demon has the thing we need to repel against the power of the tree!" she exclaimed, jabbing her pen at one of the octopus's tentacles. In the drawing, it was holding what seemed to be a blue gem. "The ocean's heart!" gasped Alex as he realised what Twylar was planning. "We need to get that heart. Soon!" she announced.

Estella informed her dad that she was leaving, he had said it would be enough time to think of handing over the army to The Legends. They were to travel to Dragon Thorn and sail all the way to the underwater cove. But they were going to do that in two days. The next day, Twylar woke up. Her back wasn't hurting as it normally did from the metal bars of her previous bed. She went outside to meet up with her friends, and they spent a few hours planning what to do the next day. Suddenly, Linda came, her nose high in the air. She brought with her a scrawny girl; her hair was all over the place, and she had huge front teeth that stuck out. There was also a girl bunny who had glasses. There were two other girls. Both of them reminded Twylar of Sammy, as they were both muscular and bulky. "Hi Linda, also, you're not coming with us." Snorted Ava, she turned her head round at began to chat with Moon.

"Well, I have my own group of friends. We were called the… Uh," she looked at her so-called friends nervously. "uhm.. The Golden Girls!" she had a smug look on her face. "Nice! You found friends who don't mind someone like you!" said Twylar sarcastically. "And the Golden Girls have declared WAR on The Legends!" laughed the scrawny girl. Suddenly,

Camilla came running up to them. "I'M THE REFEREE," she shouted, and she cleared her throat. "Alright, Golden Girls, I'll be needing your names. I already know The Legends' names." She pulled out a notebook and a pen. "Mine's Emily." Snorted one of the bulky-looking girls. "And I'm Evelyn!" shrieked the other. "I'm Diana." Said the scrawny-looking girl with a voice that seemed as if she was trying to imply she was smarter than everyone there. "And I'm carrot!" said the bunny with glasses, and she seemed to be nicer than all of them put together.

"Alrighty.. follow me to the first test!" exclaimed Camilla as she sped off. "Why are we doing this..." groaned Alex. "Yayyy, Linda has minions now.." said Twylar sarcastically, as she was being dragged without her will by Ava. Once they reached their spot (which was just a flat piece of land, there was a pool filled with water and a rope.) Camilla stood in front of them and instructed what they were going to do. "Tug of war! Powers are allowed!" she announced. She stepped aside and let them get themselves in order. The Legends were on the right, and The Golden Girls on the left. The thing is... none of The Golden Girls had powers, while all The Legends did. They got themselves ready. Moon called some wild bears over to help. Lily couldn't transform as her form was too big. Ava prepared herself as her sword was no use in this situation, and so was Alex. Twylar was at the front. She was in her dark amethyst form, her normal human ears had disappeared, and now, she had wolf ears at the top of her head.

At the other end, Linda was upfront. She insisted that as she is prettier and stronger, she goes first, not Emily or Evelyn. They were second in line, Emily being in front of Evelyn. Carrot was behind Evelyn and Diana at the back. "BEGIN" shrieked Camilla, she blew her whistle. Each team pulled and pulled, but thanks to Moon, the bears she had called were helping them to gain the win. The pool was getting dreadfully close to the other team; first, Linda fell in. She emerged, her hair and clothes drenched. "LINDA OUT! FOUR LEFT," yelled Camilla, who was doing a great job as a referee. Linda sulked as she walked over to a nearby bench and sat down.

Soon after the other, each member of 'The Golden Girls' fell into the pool. "THE LEGENDS WIN!" shrieked Camilla as soon as Diana had fallen in the pool. She started cheering, but all the winners wanted to do was plan the voyage to Dragon Thorn. Linda and her 'friends' ran over to them. They had looks of pure hatred and jealousy on their faces. "Well, next time, we'll win! We're better than you in every way! I was only being nice to you, Twylar, because I had a kind heart," Linda shrieked, and she went on rambling about how great she and her friend group were. "Yeah, I mean, look at us! We're practically rolling in gold!" bragged Emily. "And science tells me that you guys have a pea-sized brain, while mine is bigger than Mars!" boasted Diana. "ALRIGHT ENOUGH!" yelled Moon suddenly. The Legends were relieved she of all people had spoken. "WE DON'T CARE HOW RICH YOU ARE, AT LEAST ALL OF US CARE ABOUT EACH OTHER!" she shrieked.

Linda looked at her in surprise. "Exactly. Estella and Moon are like baker besties. Me and Alex help each other with our problems and Ava cares about all of us!" agreed Twylar. Suddenly, Ava stepped forward, her sword in her hand. "Listen, Linda and her nerdy friends, scram before I chop your heads off. This sword is sharp." She said menacingly. Linda took a step back, and Emily cracked her knuckles. "Also, this war's over!" added Moon. "Bye, the bratty girls!" waved Alex as he levitated all of them. "YOU'RE JUST JEALOUS!!!" yelled Linda as she floated away.

Camilla just stared. "Alright, so about Dragon Thorn," began Ava, as though nothing had happened. Camilla walked over to Twylar, bent down, and whispered in her ear. "Don't trust the captains. They lure you to your death. Yes, I know you're going to that underwater cove." she whispered. She smiled and walked back to the castle. Her black, waist-long hair shimmering under the sunlight. Twylar passed this information on to her friends, who nodded. "Ok.. this means we have to either make a boat or steal one." Concluded Lily. Alex had a very nervous look on his face. "What is it?" Twylar whispered to Alex. "Oh uh.. nothing much, I'm just sea-sick," he whispered back. The day had soon come to an end, The legends found no trace of 'The Golden Girls' but did not actually care about their whereabouts.

They were huddled in Lily's room, much to her object. "Why is it always my place? First, my own home, now my room!" she whined as she reluctantly let Moon in. Camilla brought them hot chocolate and coffee for herself. She sat next to Twylar and listened to Estella. "Basically, my dad said it's best not to bring too many people, so Camilla, you can't come. Sorry!" she apologised. Camilla smiled in response. "Well, here's my plan," began Twylar. "We all split up, Ava and me, Alex and Estella"- Alex threw Twylar a lethal look. "And Lily's with Moon." Moon nodded. "We each go separate ways to the harbour to avoid Dragon Thorn police." Ava drank the rest of her drink and put it on a table. "As you know, Dragon Thorn and Cosmic City are in an alliance with The Isle Of

Irene, so we can't get caught." She explained. "one problem, what about the boat?" asked Lily. "hmm, maybe... Estella, you can turn invisible, right?" Ava turned to face Estella. "Yeah, that's my power." She nodded. "Then you can turn invisible, bonk the captain or whoever's on board the ship and drive it!" exclaimed Ava. "Sounds good!" agreed Estella. She, too, had finished her drink. Camilla took the empty cups back downstairs and handed them to one of the servants.

With that, they each went to their rooms, but Moon had decided to sleep with her family. Twylar lay in bed, but she wanted to see her mother again now that she knew she could. She transformed into a light amethyst, and pale yellow fire emerged from her palms. Suddenly, Queen Amber was standing before her. She was still a bit pale because she was a ghost, but Twylar could see her amber eyes and her luscious blonde hair. "My child! It's been a few days since I last saw you, about 3 days, I believe." She said, her voice shaking. "Mum, what happened?" asked Twylar, noticing the shake in her mother's voice. "Well... Shavanii is known to hate werewolves and basically anything that isn't human, animal or demon." She said, her voice cracking. "He killed my father." She said. It was obvious she was reliving a terrible memory, more like a nightmare.

"Mum, it's ok! I survived my dad, and I'm pretty sure some sea demon can't even lay a finger- I mean tentacle on me!" she said reassuringly. Queen Amber smiled. Then, she disappeared as soon as Twylar had blinked. With a heavy heart, she climbed down the stairs and reached the dining room. Everyone was already there, but they were waiting for Twylar. None of them had touched their food. All members of staff were there, including the king. She sat down next to Ava and Moon, and before they dug in, the king spoke. "The kingdom of Bunny Town wishes you a safe journey to Dragon Thorn and that you safely retrieve the ocean's heart from the sea demon Shavanii. I will have made my decision when you come back." He said, in his serious voice. They began to eat without further ado. Camilla stayed with Linda back at the castle. And, after The Legends had finished eating, Estella used her powers on her friends to turn them (and herself) invisible.

After about 8 hours of travelling (They rode on the backs of horses) it had begun to get dark. They set up camp, and everyone had one to themselves but Lily had to sleep with Moon because her tent had got ripped! The next day, Lily had decided it would be easier if she transformed into a siren and held her friends in her massive hands.

Moon, however, rode on the back of a Bear, as Bunny Town forests were full of them. With the wind in her hair, Twylar stood up but was charged by a sharp gust of wind. She held onto Lily for life! They had spent the entire day travelling to Dragon Thorn. By the time they got there, it was already night!

Lily transformed back into a human and the bear that Moon had ridden rampaged off into the tangled forests of Dragon Thorn. "Alright, here's the gameplan", began Twylar, as she handed everyone long, black cloaks. "we split up. I'm with Ava, Alex is with Estella-" Alex handed Twylar a lethal look as he put on his hood. "and Lily's with Moon." Lily nodded, and she, too put on her hood. "Okay, everyone got their hoods on?" Twylar asked as she made sure her face was cloaked in darkness. They all nodded and waited for Twylar to speak. "Remember, make it to the South Harbour, that's where it's easiest to get to 'the Drowned'."

Then she and Ava bid farewell, and they went their separate ways. Before following Ava, Twylar managed to look at Alex, who couldn't even Look at Estella! "Come on! The quicker we get to the harbour, the better!" yelled Ava. Realising she was far behind, Twylar ran to catch up with her best friend. Scattered across the inky night sky were several glistening gems and a moon that was like a massive lantern. It lit the way for the two friends. Soon, they had reached the bustling markets full of busy people. The Dragon Thorn markets were all red. Suddenly, a man bumped into Twylar. "Oh, sorry!" he said quickly. "Happy Rose Regalia..." he murmured as he tried to get through. "I'm sorry, but what do you mean?" Twylar asked bluntly. "Oh? The Rose Regalia festival? We celebrate it every time our king passes away. It's also a way of celebrating our new king. Which, right now, is King Cedric. Are you a tourist?" he pointed out, observing Twylar's dark cloak that draped around her shoulders.

"Oh, uh, indeed I am! Um... have a nice day, sir!" called Twylar as she watched the man run like a headless chicken, holding his brown hat and his suitcase. Suddenly, there was silence and whispers of excited crowds. Ava was nowhere to be seen. "Twy!" hissed Ava, coming somewhere from Twylar's left. She followed the voice and ended up finding her blue-haired bestie again. "There you are!" she sighed. "Girl, I got the news. Apparently, there's this Rose Regalia festival these guys are doing, which means it'll be harder to get to the harbour without getting caught."

Announced Twylar as she hurried to the back. "Well, let's just see what this festival is about." Suggested Ava as she dragged Twylar to the front. "DEAR CITIZENS! WE HOLD THIS ROSE REGALIA FESTIVAL TODAY TO MOURN FOR THE LATE KING, HIS MAJESTY KING ARTHUR," boomed a voice. Twylar looked up and saw that a massive statue of a man was there. Underneath were huge wheels and 10 servants holding onto them. And right next to the statue was the source of the booming voice. It was just another servant, but standing next to him was a young man with messy dark brown hair and hazel, lion-like eyes. "I PRONOUNCE PRINCE CEDRIC, KING!" boomed the servant. He placed a glistening gold crown on top of King Cedric's head, which was embedded with all sorts of beauties.

Twylar saw his greedy face. He looked as though he did not care that his father had just passed away. "I'd also like to make an announcement." He drawled, his voice silky and posh. "Sounds like a narcissist. Acts like a narcissist." Whispered Ava to Twylar, who was cloaking her entire face in darkness out of fear that anyone might recognise her black burn mark. Suddenly, Cedric's hazel, lion-like eyes stared at Twylar. She felt a cold shiver run down her spine. "I know my... father.. hated King William, but now I'm king. Things are going to be a lot different," he smirked. "Dragon Thorn, Cosmic City, and The Isle Of Irene have made one big alliance with each other. We call it 'The Unified League' or TUL." He stared at Twylar as though trying to remember something. "So, from now on, I urge you to report any sightings of the demon princess, Twylar Irene and her rebellious friends." He stepped back and let his servant do the talking. "ENJOY YOUR ROSE REGALIA FESTIVAL EVERYONE, AND A HAPPY ROSE REGALIA TO YOU!" boomed the servant. He stumbled to get into the carriage, but Cedric stopped him. "royalty first." He smiled as he pushed the servant aside. As soon as the carriage sped off, people started throwing what seemed like rose petals at the statue. Twylar immediately understood the statue was meant to look like Dragon Thorn's dead king, and she understood why people were throwing rose petals at it. "I get it, Ava. The Rose Regalia festival is just the dead king's funeral and a celebration of the new king." Whispered Twylar. "Twy! There's a guy over there trying to steal those cookies," Ava hissed, ignoring Twylar. "Okay... and?" shrugged Twylar. "There's a reason why I became a royal guard you know!" said Ava as she sped off towards the young man stealing the cookies. "Ava, wait!" pleaded Twylar as she ran after her reluctantly. The man jumped, shoved a few cookies into his pocket and ran off with Ava high on his tail. "WE'RE SUPPOSED TO BE AT THE HARBOUR BY NOWW!" shouted Twylar as she chased after Ava. The chase went on, and luckily, Ava had the man cornered. "Wha' d'you wan'?" he said, his mouth bursting with cookies. "Give back those cookies! Stealing is wrong!" commanded Ava. "Ha! You thin' I'll give deez back?" He sprayed cookie crumbs from his mouth in every direction. "Ew... I'm allergic to boys... hurry up and finish the ones in your mouth, and I'll grab the ones you haven't touched." Ava acted as though she was about to vomit. The man seemed hurt. He swallowed and opened his mouth to speak. "I have a name y'know! It's Zilas..." he said in a hurt voice. "Stop acting like a baby. Hurry up and give me the rest of those cookies." Commanded Ava. "What is going on, Ava... WE'RE SUPPOSED TO BE AT THE HARBOURRRR!" shrieked Twylar. She grabbed her head tightly.

"HAH, I AIN'T EVER GIVING DEEZ BACK!!" shouted Zilas, as he fished out the remaining cookies from his pocket and shoved them in his mouth. "Well, if you're going to be like that, then at least tell us about Shavanii." Said Ava, in a voice that Twylar knew ever so well. "S-SHAVANII!?" whimpered Zilas as he looked around. "Stop acting as if Shavanii's Voldemort because it's not." Sighed Ava, she slapped her forehead. "V-V-VOLDEMORT!?????" he shrieked, getting more terrified. "He's more useless than Alex..." murmured Ava quietly to herself. "Why's he screaming? He does know old Voldy's not real?" whispered Twylar to Ava. "HE IS!" said Zilas angrily as he overheard their conversation. "Uh huh, anyway, tell us how to get to the south harbour unnoticed!" smiled Twylar as she stepped forward.

She looked at Zilas; he had messy, curly black hair, and a red bandana was covering his forehead. He had icy blue eyes but Twylar could tell he was just a goofy, silly guy. "Ok, fine! Follow me." He jumped onto his feet and ran off. Ava chased after him. "Yesterday's enemy is today's ally..." said Twylar in an undertone to Ava. They followed Zilas and he had not let them down. Waiting impatiently were the rest of The Legends, who asked all at once where they had been. "Ok, uhm, everyone, meet Zilas! He uhm tell us about yourself!" said Twylar, awkwardly. "Um, I'm from Dragon Thorn",- he began. "We know that, but ok" interrupted Moon. "I'm a good fighter uhm, my dad gave me this thingy," he pointed to his red bandana. "Aaaand that's it." He finished. Ava raised her eyebrows and could not help herself. "Oh, same! I'm also a very good fighter, WAIT!" she paused, "YOU COULD HELP US DEFEAT SHAVANII!!!" she screamed. "Ok.." he agreed reluctantly. "Wait, so is this guy in The

Legends?" asked Alex. "Yeah, I guess..." confirmed Ava. "Yay?" questioned Zilas, not knowing what 'The Legends' was. "Well, I can just transform into a siren and swim to the cove, but y'all can't breathe underwater!" exclaimed Lily as she got ready to jump into the murky depths of the sea. "Wait... HOW ARE YOU A SIREN!??" shouted Zilas, backing away from Lily. "Oh yeah... just don't question the letter that's gonna come for you when you get your powers." Explained Moon. "Yeah, those time-telling letters!" agreed Estella. Zilas just stared in bewilderment. They managed to steal a boat, and Lily was pushing it underwater as there were no oars. (they had stolen a cruise and thrown the captain off-board)

Everyone was doing their own thing. The baker besties were in the kitchen (surprisingly, the ship had one!). They were baking some cupcakes for the journey. Zilas and Ava practised their skills and showed them off to each other. Ava was quite impressed with Zilas! "Okay... Moon and Estella are baker besties... Zilas and Ava are sword besties?" wondered Twylar. Meanwhile, Lily was having fun splashing everyone with her massive siren tail. "Don't question it," blurted out Ava, as Lily had sent a tsunami headed Zilas's way. He gulped. "I HATE THE WATERR!!" he screamed as the cold water hit him. Alex and Twylar were looking out for Lily and would hide behind barrels whenever she came close.

"We're so smart", whispered Alex as he hid behind a large, wooden barrel. "Yeah", agreed Twylar as Lily continued to search for them. "I'll find you, Twy and Alex, and when I do, THE BIGGEST STUNAMI THERE EVER WAS WILL BE HEADING YOUR WAY!!" Lily screamed irritably.

Lily went off and headed towards the direction of Moon and Estella. She transformed into a human and, followed by the smell of hot pastries, led herself towards the kitchen. Zilas was in the middle of sword fighting with Ava (they were using wooden sticks) when his letter came. He caught it floating towards him, curiosity guiding him. He grabbed the letter, and Ava urged the rest of The Legends to come. The letter read: "Dear Zilas Davidson, I'm sure the rest of The Legends are familiar with this, except for Estella and Alex, but your time has come. Here are your two powers that have been gifted to you today; they were given to you in aid of your fighting abilities. (I'm not saying it's bad) You have the ability to create barriers around you or your friends. Nothing can break through it. And, just like with Twylar's flames, you can shoot out a surge of blue energy that could burn through anything. Signed, the watcher."

Zilas stared at it and turned it over in hopes of something else that would explain this to him. "Ooo nice! I can turn invisible! I was born with this power, though.." complimented Estella. Ava stared suspiciously at her friends and realised one person was missing. "SURPRISE ATTACK!!!" yelled Lily from behind. They were all standing at the front of the massive cruise, and there was a pool, too! The tsunami that Lily had made with her tail was far bigger than any of her previous ones; it was enough to drown in! Suddenly, without thinking, the letter's words proved true as Zilas closed his eyes in concentration. When he reopened them, he saw the faint outline of Lily. She was laughing her heart out, it was like he was in a glass tunnel at the aquarium. There was a faint, white circle around him and Ava; she touched it gently with the tip of her finger.

"Woah! So, this is the barrier the watcher was talking about! Wondered Ava out loud. Zilas could hear the screams and shouts of Estella and Moon, the snorts of laughter from Lily as she watched the cruise get flooded, but where were Twylar and Alex? You know how I said the entire cruise was flooded? Well, I was kind of wrong. There was a bit at the top, which was unharmed, and on top of that were Twylar and Alex. "TRUE LEGENDS ALWAYS SURVIVE!" she yelled, making sure to rub it in Lily's face. She was in her werewolf form, her big black wings nestled comfortably behind her, and she still had anxiety about the loss of her human ears when she transformed into a werewolf. Alex used his levitating powers on himself and was struggling to come down from high in the sky. In the end, he managed it. "GUYS I'M HARRY POTTAH!!" he joked. He stuck his tongue out at Lily, who stared at him with pure hatred. Or annoyance. The line between them was very blurry at this moment. They could see from the top of the cruise that Estella was holding onto whatever she could find, and Moon's screams were drowned out by the water and the shouts for help from Estella.

Lily lifted the cruise with ease, and shook it gently at first so that her friends could get off, then she shook it hard so all the water was gone. When they clambered back in, they found it was very damp, and there were puddles everywhere. The bad thing is that the pool was no longer filled with water. Ava, Zilas, Twylar and Alex were unscathed, though Estella and Moon were drenched in cold, salty seawater. Estella hurried inside, relieved to find that the indoors were only a bit damp. She ran to the fireplace and huddled near it. "UGH, LILY, WHY WOULD YO-" began Moon before thinking of a more evil thought.

51

A smile lingered on her face as she thought of the evil thing she was about to do. What she was going to do would surely make King William seem... almost ALMOST human. "Ava, Twy, Alex and Zilas get behind me now, or if you'd rather follow Estella, be my guest." Grunted Moon. Twylar stayed with Moon but ran inside to get popcorn, knowing that something was about to go down. Realising the signs, Ava stayed with Moon too. It was only the boys who went to the fireplace. "CREATURES OF THE SALTY SEA, COME FORTH, MY FRIENDS- AND ATTACK THE GIRL! DO NOT HARM MYSELF OR THE GIRLS BEHIND ME!!" she yelled, her voice echoing in every direction. Lily, with her eyebrows raised, transformed into a human and clambered onto the damp cruise. Forgetting all about Moon's animal-controlling power. Suddenly, the animals responded and out-jumped sharks of all sizes with intimidating teeth. Jellyfish obeyed Moon and made their way onto the cruise. Some starfish came along, too, and they all started attacking poor Lily. They pulled at her dark brown, braided hair and gnawed at her dark skin. One massive shark flopped towards her and bit deep into her leg. "GET IT OFF, GET IT OFF, MOON!!" she shrieked, running around like a headless chicken. "PLEASEEE MOON, I WON'T SPLASH YOU AGAIN!" she pleaded. Moon, deciding that Lily had learnt her lesson, raised her arms and spoke. "MY WATERY FRIENDS, YOU HAVE DONE ENOUGH! BE GONE! LIVE YOUR NORMAL FISHY LIVES!" she shrieked, and on her word, every sea creature retreated -flopped- back to their homes. The shark left Lily's leg, leaving a massive wound. Something warm was trickling down her leg.

Moon gave Lily a death stare and went inside to join the rest of The Legends. Twylar, knowing she was the only one with the ability to heal, rushed to Lily. She transformed into a light amethyst and healed Lily within seconds. Alex happened to be at the doorstep, watching all of what had just happened. "Moon's nice, but... I don't ever want to get her angry..." murmured Alex. Twylar finished all her popcorn and nodded darkly. They joined their friends inside, near the fireplace. Lily retold the shark incident to the others, but to everyone that day, Moon was a hero.

"Remember, don't splash us, or baby shark's gonna go; baby shark do-do-do baby shark bites you", said Moon fiercely. Just then, Estella returned with the cupcakes the baker's besties had baked earlier. Lily had a cupcake with a fish theme to it, seeing as she was a siren. Twylar had purple frosting, and an edible picture of herself was on it. Estella had a pink frosting one with an edible bunny and carrot on it. Alex had a dark purple one with miniature stars and bits of what seemed to be distant galaxies. Zilas had a red cupcake with an image of a sword on it, Ava too. Moon's was also pink; she had an image of herself on it, like Twylar's. "Oh right, I forgot I dyed permanent pink into my hair," realised Moon as she was standing in front of a mirror. Her pigtails were always the same, her hair light brown and fading into it at the bottom was light pink. "Mmm, that was good, but I need to go drive the cruise now!" exclaimed Lily, completely forgetting about the shark incident.

"Lily, can you refill the pool?" asked Estella. Lily did a thumbs-up and jumped off the cruise. She emerged as a giant siren. With cupped hands, she refilled the pool, but she refilled it a little bit too much! Estella jumped into the pool, her pink, wavy hair all over the place. Moon joined in, too, followed by Zilas. Twylar and Alex were near the pool, but Alex was staring at Estella. "Go talk to her", whispered Twylar, elbowing Alex in the ribs. "I can't. Are you dumb?" he asked savagely. "Perfect time to use those pixel sunglasses I bought from Dragon Thorn!" thought Twylar excitedly. "At least I'm not a mistake," Twylar fished out her sunglasses and put them on. She turned her back and walked away. Alex just stood there, realising he got violated. He tried to think of a comeback, but in the end, he joined the already full pool. "Um... it's kinda packed in here.." he murmured, figuring he couldn't even move or get out!

Twylar stood at the rooftop, the spot she'd been when she escaped Lily's tsunami. She transformed into a light amethyst and played with her yellow flames. Suddenly, she found herself in the white nothingness again. "Mum? What happened now?" she asked, turning to face her mother. "You've seen those letters, yes? From the watcher?" she asked. "Yeah, Zilas just got his letter." Answered Twylar. "I am the watcher. There are things I cannot tell

you just yet, and how you get your powers, but I am the one that writes it to you. So that you know." She confessed. "Why am I not surprised.. after everything that's happened... IN EXACTLY ONE MONTH," she yelled angrily. "I know, me getting murdered, the fire, Camilla's escape, the 3 newest members of The Legends," she continued. "Soon, the world will know you and your friends as real legends. If you save the circle of kingdoms, you have also saved the world from what possibly would seem like war.." her eyes fixated on Twylar. "Just know, my child, you may have to face your dear old dad sooner than you think-"those were the last words she heard before she was whisked away into reality. "the white nothingness.. again?" asked Ava. "Wait, how did you get onto the roof?" said Twylar, realising there was no ladder. "Alex made me float. It was for a prank, and now I'm here." She drawled. Her mind seemed elsewhere like she was thinking deeply about something. Suddenly, Lily emerged from the water. She looked worn out. She transformed into a human. Twylar flew down with her impressive wings, and she carried Ava down, too. "Guys.. we're here… I don't think I can come… all that pushing…" she fell to the ground. Moon carried her inside and got ready to dive into the sea. "Stop Moon! The cove's a long way down there, and we can't breathe underwater like Lily!" reasoned Estella. "Plus, I'm gonna stay with Lily, make sure she's alright." She huffed and went to the room Lily was in. "no problem! I can make a barrier around us!" said Zilas, prepared to jump. Everyone dived into the murky depths of the endless sea. Zilas had made a barrier around them. Realising they could breathe again, Moon summoned some dolphins to quickly carry them to the cove. Still, the journey on the cruise took about 2 days, and the journey to the actual cove took about 8 hours. They were already half asleep when they reached the cove! They noticed a strange, blue light emitting from the inside. Twylar was the first to go in, followed by Ava and the rest. When they entered, they found the small cove was roomy and spacious on the inside.

The strange light seemed to be coming from… "Shavanii" whispered Twylar. The sea demon was a huge octopus, the light was coming from it. "Ok, me and Zilas distract Shavanii whilst you guys try to find the heart," announced Ava. "W-why us!?" trembled Zilas. Twylar nodded. Moon and Alex followed her in search of the ocean's heart. The thing they came so long for. The thing they need to win this war. "All or nothing…" thought Ava. She jumped onto the back of the sea demon. "Wait… there's air down here… how can Shavanii breathe?" thought Ava. "Because I'm a sea demon, it runs in my blood." Shavanii had the ancient voice of an old man. Twylar saw it's many teeth, all round the inside of its neck and on its mouth, too. "Prepare to DIE!!" it shrieked. It grabbed Ava by her leg and dangled her above his head. Without thinking, Zilas shot the blue energy out of his palms. It burned through Shavanii's tentacles, and Ava was free from its grasp. She quickly climbed back up the steep walls to the entrance and brandished her sword. She managed to cut another of its tentacles off, slimy.. stuff began oozing out of it.

Meanwhile, with Twylar, she was having trouble finding the heart. She did not know what it looked like, so how was she supposed to find it? Meanwhile, back with Zilas and Ava, "I HATE THISSSSSSS!!!!" squealed Zilas as he ran away from Shavanii. "Oh, come on!" urged Ava as she defended herself against the sea demon's slimy tentacles. Suddenly, as he stole a glance at Ava, he accidentally slipped and fell. He thought that was the end of him. the end of his painful life. But no. He was hanging off a rocky cliff, and underneath him was Shavanii. His mouth was open wide, ready for Zilas to drop into his mouth.

"ZILAS HOLD ON!" screamed Ava, as she rushed to grab his hand. She tried to pull him up, but she couldn't. "I'VE FOUND IT GUYS, IT'S LIKE A BLUE SORT OF THINGY!!" yelled Alex as Twylar tried to reach the heart. Whilst Zilas was in danger of being eaten, they had found the heart in the spot where the sea demon was. It was the heart that was emitting the strange, blue light! Twylar tried to reach it, but she couldn't risk falling. See, the heart was floating above what seemed like a bottomless hole, but when they looked down, they could only see darkness.

After Twylar had failed, Moon tried her best too but she still could not reach it. Alex, who was a bit taller than both Twylar and Moon, managed to just touch it with his fingertips. "make sure not to drop it in the hole!" advised Moon. She had just noticed the danger Zilas was in, and it looked like Shavanii was getting impatient. "wait.. I'm so dumb... I CAN MAKE MYSELF FLOAT!!" laughed Alex as he floated towards the heart. He grabbed it and held it close to his chest. When he came back down, they immediately made their way towards Zilas and Ava. " WE FOUND IT!! THE OCEAN'S HEART!!" yelled Alex, showing it to Ava.

Twylar held Ava's free hand, Moon held Twylar's, and Alex held onto Moon. "Y'ALL PULL!!" commanded Moon. They became a human chain, and in the end, managed to save Zilas's life. "let's get out of-" began Alex, before getting interrupted by the angry roar of Shavanii. "yeah, let's get out of here! Zilas, the barrier?" asked Ava quickly. Zilas formed a white barrier around them, and they were able to breathe underwater.

When they returned back to their cruise, they realized it had been at least 24 hours they had been there! They hurried inside to check on Lily and Estella. They found them both in one of the bedrooms the cruise had, Lily was lying in her bed, and Estella was right by her side. "wow... Estella's so caring! She's the bunny princess, alright!" wondered Twylar in her mind. After they had retrieved the ocean's heart, they all came together to take a closer look.

It seemed to be alive, as it looked like it was pulsing. The blue light lit up the starry skies. Lily emerged from the water. She looked worn out as she transformed back into a human. She grunted as a hello and walked over to the heart. As soon as her fingers touched it, her eyebags disappeared, her hair wasn't messy, and she looked as if she had a good night's sleep. "Wait... Lily is a siren.. this is the ocean's heart.. siren is part of the sea.. WAIT A MINUTE!!" realised Zilas; he pointed at the heart, then at Lily. "LILY GRAB THE HEART AND TRANSFORMMM!" he commanded, practically itching in excitement. Lily grabbed the heart, clung it to her chest, and jumped into the water. As soon as she had emerged from the water, something looked different. Instead of a scaly green tail, her tail was still green, but it had a glowing, light blue design embedded in it. Same with every part of her body, her clothes were ripped from transforming, and her hair was illuminating the night sky. From her usual dark skin, her skin had turned sort of greenish, but you could tell deep down it was Lily.

She seemed so excited she could sing! She began to hum at first before getting interrupted. "LILY DON'T SING! YOU'RE A SIREN. YOU'LL KILL US!" warned Twylar, clasping her hands to her ears. Lily closed her mouth and sang no more, though she tried to look for the heart. Had she lost it? Certainly not! She touched her forehead, and the blue heart was right there, sunken deep beneath her skin. "cool!" she breathed. She transformed back into a human and found that the glistening blue heart was still on her forehead. "Well.. that's good that means no one can steal it!" remarked Estella as she took a closer look.

Lily slept in her bed later that night. She touched the thing on her forehead. The ocean's heart. It was pulsing gently now, in rhythm with her own heart. The next day, Lily began work and transformed. She dived into the sea and pushed the cruise, but to her surprise, she was much faster than before! To her, the ocean was her friend. Her home. Kind of like Moana, except Lily was a siren. They made it back to Dragon Thorn quicker than expected, all thanks to Lily. The Legends sneaked past the guards on patrol and saw King Cedric there, too. In the end, Lily transformed into a siren, with legs. She carried her friends and ran. She ran all the way back to Bunny Town. That took about 1 hour to do.

When they reached the gates of the bunny castle, all the bunnies stopped and stared. Lily put down her friends and transformed back into a human. Later that evening, the bunny king invited The Legends to a dinner party to celebrate the defeat of Shavanii and the retrieval of the ocean's heart. Once they arrived, they sat down. Alex was just wearing a fancy dinner suit, and so was Zilas, but he was uncomfortable in it. Twylar was wearing a sparkly purple dress, Estella had a white headband placed upon her wavy pink hair, and she wore a pink dress with a white, puffy coat on top. Lily, known to all her friends as the fashion queen, was wearing a leopard print dress, also with a puffy white coat. Moon was the last to come, so they began without her. They were halfway into their meal when Moon finally arrived. Everyone turned their heads but was surprised to see Moon without her usual pigtails. Right now, she had curled them nicely, and she brought them upfront. The pinkish colour at the bottom of her hair faded into her natural brown hair.

She was wearing a white bow just like Ava's (the one she lost back in The Isle Of Irene). Her dress was a minty colour and she was wearing very high, black heels. She even had some makeup put on! Her lips were as red as a rose, and her eyelashes were plastered with mascara. "Ok, uhm, you kinda ruined the makeup I gave you, but the outfit is slaying," remarked Lily as she stood up and started clapping. Soon followed by the rest. "Why are y'all clapping!?" asked Moon as she sat down next to Twylar. "Because you always look ugly and nerdy, and now that you had a glow-up, we gotta clap!" snorted Ava as she came through the door. Her light blue hair was not tied, and she was wearing a white dress. She sat down next to Lily. "Well, you two are 10 minutes late, but that's alright!" said the bunny king, with a voice that indicated he was already tired. "Let the feast-for the second time, begin!" he announced. He stumbled to get back to his chair. After they had finished their meals, the dinner party had ended. The girls, who were too lazy to take off their dresses, just stood outside and stared at the moon. (they weren't staring at Moon, you know, the actual person?) the boys, however, gladly took off their suits and flopped onto their beds. (Zilas flopped onto the couch; he sleeps there because there wasn't an extra room) Camilla ran up to Twylar and gave her the biggest hug. Linda and her circle of friends were yet to be found, and the most important thing... they had a heart.

Suddenly, whilst outside, the bunny king came up to them. He was about the height of a toddler, seeing as he's a bunny. More like a rabbit, as bunnies are baby rabbits! "I have made my decision. You can have my army." He announced. And with that, he swiftly left the room (sorry, I mean the balcony). All the girls looked at one another in surprise. They decided to change into normal clothes and take off their makeup. The legends said goodnight to each other and headed off to their rooms to sleep.

The next day, Ava sent one of the bunny agents to The Isle Of Irene in hopes of something useful, like when King William was going to go to the spirit forest. When the bunny agent came back, he confirmed that King William was going in 2 weeks' time, so The Legends decided to go in 1 week. They pretty much did nothing, though Lily and Moon did go to the nearby beach to take a look at Lily's new powers. "it's kinda freaky, though... what would it look like if the heart thingy was stabbed? Would the ocean die or something?" commented Moon as she pointed at Lily's forehead. Lily, who had become a siren, lifted Moon up. "hey! P-put me d-down! You know I hate heights!!" she pleaded, as she wearily looked down, only to see the roaring ocean below her.

Lily smiled and lowered her a little. Though she was still high in the air. "chill out, I'm just gonna show you something!" she giggled as Lily walked over the sea with ease. (she had transformed into a siren with green, scaly legs) the walk took hardly one minute, and they were at their destination already. "Ta-da!" Lily put Moon down on a small island before transforming into a human. "It's a picnic!" she giggled as she sat down near the basket. It was nearly sunrise, and the picnic was facing the way that the sun would rise.

They both sat down and enjoyed a quantity of jam doughnuts and sandwiches with fresh lemonade on the side. As the sunrise fell onto them, the two best friends forgot about everything. "Well, we already had breakfast. Let's go wake the others up," suggested Moon as she got up and dusted herself with her hands. She packed the picnic up and allowed Lily to carry her across the raging sea. She gulped and tried not to look down, though she couldn't help herself. Once they made it back, they woke up the rest of their friends and got yelled at for waking them up so early; the news reached them that 'The Golden Girls' were found. "oh, it's the losers again. DIANAAA!!!" screamed Linda as soon as her eyes met Twylar's. "yeah?" questioned Diana. "What is the percentage of 'The Legends' being losers?" she smirked. "Based on my non-bias calculation, science tells me that based on their personality, The Legends' percentage of being losers would be approximately 34%, but if I round it by 10 and multiply the answer by 12..." she rambled on and on about useless math equations and summaries, before Linda concluded that their percentage of being losers was 100%. "And since The Golden Girls are so amazing, we don't feel any need to be living in a... dumpster, like this palace." Boasted Linda as she trotted off towards the woods. Her minions followed her. "Ughh, why'd she have to come back..." groaned Moon. "She's giving me a migraine already.." moaned Ava

"Uhm, what's The Golden Girls?" asked Zilas. In the middle of the woods, Linda and her minions hacked through overgrown grass and roots of trees that could potentially trip them over. "Alright, The Legends must be shown that The Golden Girls are superior to them!" said Linda as she rested on a tree stump. "Well, they've battled a sea demon, fought King William, pretty much the main characters, while we rot as the extras." Concluded Diana, pushing her glasses up her nose. "So maybe we fight King William too? Let's just go to The Isle Of Irene!" snorted Emily. Evelyn nodded her head. "I don't know, guys.. but it would be nice to be the main character once in a while.." whimpered Carrot. Everyone ignored poor Carrot and agreed with Emily. "Okay, EVERYONE! MAKE A BOAT!!" commanded Linda.

And so, everyone started collecting branches and sticks and slowly made a raft big enough for all of them. Evelyn and Emily were rowing the boat with sticks to The Isle Of Irene, and Diana had made an anchor with the necessary equations and mathematical assumptions needed to make it. They had spent all day travelling to The Isle Of Irene, and they weren't even half-way there! Diana let down the anchor, and soon everyone drifted off into an uncomfortable sleep. When they woke up, they were hungry but they couldn't eat anything, as they had nothing to catch fish with, and nothing to cook the food. "we'd better get there soon or we'll die of hunger!" said Carrot, as she nervously nibbled at her paws. So everyone helped row the boat, all except for Linda. When they finally made it to The Isle Of Irene, they stole a bit of bread from a bakery, they saw Sunset café, but there was no hungry swarms of people surrounding it. After the fire, everything seemed perfectly normal. Thanks to King William's magic, the kingdom was repaired in no time!

Linda tore off the biggest bit of bread, and gave her friends a tiny crumb. "alright, now let's sneak into the castle!" said Evelyn, excitedly. When they reached the mighty blue castle, the white pillars outside the light blue concrete walls held carvings of the first Irenes who inhabited this kingdom, the blue turrets fluttering in the wind, this castle surely was the greatest thing man had ever built! They couldn't just enter through the main gate, they would instantly get caught! So Diana, being the smarty pants of the group, devised a plan. "so me and Carrot will distract the guards who patrol the castle, once we distract them Evelyn will knock them out, and Emily will sneak into the castle, and unlock the door." She said, staring deeply into her friends' souls. "actually, I'll be the one to sneak into the castle-" began Linda, as she applied some lipstick to her already colourful lips. "huh.. anyone here?" asked one of the guards, everyone kept quiet behind the bushes they were hiding behind. Once he had left, the girls formed their plan. Diana pretended to be a lonely orphan, and Carrot her pet bunny to gather the guard's attention. Evelyn bonked the guard heavily with her fists on his head, he fell to the floor. "lil' too hard?" she asked, innocently. Much to Linda's object, Emily was the one to sneak into the castle, she broke in through an open window and let in her friends.

Linda grunted, and was about to make a fuss when they heard something: it sounded like two girls giggling.. they immediately took cover, and made sure no one could see them. "so glad our demon sister's gone! I mean, it's only been 5 weeks but we're still celebrating!" laughed Stacey. "yeah, let's go to the mall tomorrow with Sammy" drawled Christie. "oh and, Twylar was never my sister" she sneered. "me too, well good thing dad's gonna go to the spirit forest in like, 2 weeks!" said Stacey, as she opened a fresh bag of crisps.

The Golden Girls looked at each other in awe and horror. Right in front of them were Princesses Christie and Stacey, but if they got caught now they would never make it back alive! Quickly, Linda crawled over to the trophy room, which was on their right. They made it in unnoticed "guys, let's steal some stuff to prove to The Legends that we did break in here!" suggested Linda, her smug face indicating all credit would be handed down to her. Everyone grabbed whatever their eyes peered down upon, Linda held a massive gold crown, she placed it atop her head. Carrot held a silver spoon, encrusted with rose-red rubies. Diana had scientifically chosen an emerald ring, whilst Emily and Evelyn were arguing over a gold sceptre. "y'know what, fine have the stupid thing I'll take this wonderful old pot.. what even is this?" snapped Evelyn, as her greedy hands grabbed a small, clay pot. Inside the pot were a stash of diamonds and rubies, and other precious crystals. Including amethysts. They made their escape and ran all the way over to their dreaded raft, though Diana had stolen a few pieces of bread from the bakery.

They stashed their stolen goods on one pile, and the bread on another. Linda held onto her crown though, saying that she deserved to wear it as she was the prettiest. When they finally arrived back at Bunny Town, the smug look on their faces and the nervous look on Carrot's brought them to the bunny castle field. The Legends were certainly shocked to see that The Golden Girls were carrying literal gold, but at the same time didn't really care.

Ava slapped her forehead and groaned. "ok? You stole from The Isle Of Irene, well done! we battled Shavanii, almost defeated King William, helped Camilla break free from her prison AND we escaped a blazing fire." Snorted Twylar. Moon, who absolutely loathed Linda, went all beast mode on her little gang. "SO? WE DON'T CARE THAT YOU MANAGED TO STEAL A BIT GOLD, WE WOULDN'T CARE IF YOU HAD A HEART ATTACK AND DIED RIGHT NOW-" she began "and she's off.." murmured Alex "there's no stopping her.." whispered Twylar. "YOU NEED TO UNDERSTAND NO ONE CARES ABOUT A BRATTY SPOILED GIRL, 2 GIRLS WHO LOOK LIKE ALL MUSCLES AND NO BRAIN, A RABBIT WHO IS SEEMINGLY NICE AND DOESN'T DESERVE ALL THIS AND SOME NERDY SMARTY PANTS WHO THINKS SHE'S SMARTER THAN EVERYONE!!!" Moon screamed. The silence was unbearable. Soon, it was Linda's turn for the shouting. "HAHAHAHAHAHAH" she laughed, hysterically. "you really think we'd rot as the extras, while you lot had all the fun as the main characters?" she sneered.

Twylar gave her 'the look' and opened her mouth to speak "ok.. Linda, you really think we're in some kind of movie? Life isn't all about cameras and fame y'know!" said Twylar, as she walked off in the opposite direction. The rest of her friends followed, except for Ava. Her light blue hair was messy and curly, and swayed because of the wind. "Linda, The Legends declare war on The Golden Girls. I don't know why I'm saying this, in my opinion it seems childish but I REALLY wanna see you lose" and with that, Ava turned on her heels and ran to catch up with her friends.

Zilas, who had happened to turn around, had seen Linda's livid face. "what exactly did you say to her?" he asked, as Ava walked alongside him. "it's war." She mumbled. When they reached Bunny bakery, they went inside. Moon closed the shop so they had privacy, and they began to talk. "Ava.. I mean you're right it would be nice to see Linda lose but what about Carrot? She seems nice!" reasoned Alex, as he sat down on a chair. "well it's Carrot's fault for being in their stupid gang." Ava said, as she slurped down her coffee. "AIN'T NO WAY YOU GUYS DO BOBA HERE!?" interrupted Twylar, as she greedily snatched the menu from Moon's hand. "obviously, it's a carrot themed one though.." confirmed

Estella, as she brought Lily her doughnuts. "man I thought back in Sunset Café would be the last time I ever saw boba.. BUT I'M WRONG GIMME SOME CARROT BOBA!!" she yelled, she accidentally wacked Lily's doughnuts onto the floor in her excitement.

Lily gave Twylar the look of nightmares, as she ate the remaining doughnuts still on her plate. Estella grabbed the doughnuts from the floor and put them in a bin, whilst Moon walked swiftly behind the counter to get Twylar her carrot themed boba. Once Twylar was handed her drink, she gulped it all down in one go and instantly requested for more. "Jam doughnuts, boba, oh man... and mochi... they're my favourite foods!!" said Twylar, as she greedily snatched her second boba from Moon.

Alex stared at Twylar with a confused look in his eyes, "uhm.. what's mochi?" he asked. "it's a Japanese dessert and it's THE BEST!!" she answered. "to be honest.. all I ever drink is coffee, sometimes good ol' boba can be good too" commented Ava, as she finally finished her coffee. Soon, everyone randomly began sharing their favourite foods and drinks, "in my opinion, apple pies are THE best!" pointed out Alex. "as you can tell, I LOVE doughnuts! I don't care what kind, jam doughnuts or plain doughnuts with no icing!" commented Lily.

Estella stared at everyone, "well growing up with bunnies kinda make you go vegan so.." she murmured. "alright you fatties, let's stop talking about food now." Joked Moon, as she sat down next to Twylar. "I'm not-" began Zilas, before getting interrupted by Ava "she didn't mean it Z," said Ava, annoyed. They began planning when they were going to go to the spirit forest, before thinking about Willow. Their ex-best friend. "still can't believe after everything we've been through, she'd choose da- I mean King William over us.." mumbled Twylar, as she remembered little Twylar and little Willow, defending her against Stacey, Christie and Sammy. "why don't you just say dad?" asked Zilas.

"well he ain't no dad to me.. he's a terrible one too" she answered, her voice stained with disgust. "well.. what are we going to do about the war that AVA declared?" said Alex, as he stared at her angrily. "bro it ain't my fault, I mean I would like to see that barbie lose.." she said, pitifully. "alright, here's the gameplan: what we're going to do is to get everyone, and I mean everyone in this kingdom to hate The Golden Girls." Began Twylar, as she leant closer and made sure no one from outside could lip read her words.

Everyone listened attentively, "and for that we need gossip. Which is what girls were made for, while we spread the gossip Zilas and Alex go up front, pretend to perform an act or something in front of a crowd, somehow bring Linda there and make it look like she was yelling at you." Whispered Twylar. Zilas and Alex nodded and listened to her. "once the girls get some people to hate them we'll beg for them to tell family and friends so that the message spreads. Alex, you'll need to distract The Golden Girls over the few couple of days so they don't notice anything. You too, Zilas." Twylar whispered. And with that, the master gameplan was born. Twylar, Moon, Ava and Lily spread the message that Linda hates kids, (all the mothers of Bunny Town now hate her) and that Evelyn and Emily eat bunnies. (everyone now stays 10 miles away from the gruesome two) they had told them to warn their family and friends, and that is what the people (bunnies) did.

Zilas and Alex invited everyone to the town square, saying they were performing a comedy act or something. Linda came along too and they had persuaded her to say some really mean things, saying that she'll get famous for it and everyone would think she was really nice and funny, guess what. The idiot believed it. Instead of everyone laughing, they were staring at poor Linda. Zilas fake cried whilst Alex pretended to comfort him.

"YOU NEED TO LEAVE!!" shouted one bunny, soon followed by the rest. Ashamed of herself, Linda ran away to her friends, who comforted her saying that the civilians didn't know what they were saying, and they should bow before a queen like her. Zilas and Alex ran away too, before they burst into fits of laughter, explaining through tears of joy what had happened. Zilas and Alex did distract The Golden Girls, which led them to believing nothing strange was going on. Even Diana couldn't figure it out!

Over the next few days, the girls had been spreading gossip whilst the boys distracted The Golden Girls, soon it was time that they confronted her- "no! not yet!!" hissed Ava, as she nudged Twylar in the ribs. Twylar rubbed the spot where it hurt, and threw Ava 'the look' she nudged her back. "let's confront her tomorrow, okay?" Said Moon, as she separated the two. "ok.." murmured Twylar and Ava. After one day of gossiping, they finally managed to get everyone's attention, and they brought The Golden Girls to the stage. Once everyone laid their eyes on them, they started booing.

"THEY EAT BUNNIES!!" yelled one nervous civilian, "THEY HATE KIDS!!" roared an angry mother. The yelling and shouting went on and on, before The Golden Girls realised that this was The Legends' doing. "UGH!!" yelled Linda, as she ran off, her friends followed. The Legends ran off too, Zilas and Ava were laughing their heads off, Estella and Moon sneered at them, though Estella was too kind and felt kind of bad. Alex and Twylar were mimicking Linda's run, making it more silly and goofy with each go. Lily was joining in too, saying that Linda ran like a headless chicken.

At the end of the day, The Golden Girls were nowhere to be seen, and The Legends were partying in Ava's room. "bro.. we're gonna be up all night.." yawned Alex, as he slurped down his drink. "yeah.. in that case I'm going to bed night guys!" agreed Twylar, as she left the room and entered hers. As she slept, her mind kept racing back to the image of her father. She was going to face him soon, but would she return alive?

The next day, she was relieved to find it was Wednesday. "only 2 more days until I get to see.. him" thought Twylar, darkly. She got dressed and quickly ate her breakfast, she rushed outside to meet her friends. Who welcomed her, with a warm smile. It was only the beginning of Winter but the trees were caked in snow, the branches had fallen off but only the trees that keep their leaves during Winter survived. The pathway was bombarded with heavy carpets of snow, and bunnies with shovels in their paws dug paths for passers-by. "ready?" asked Ava, "yeah!" replied Twylar.

So, they began their day out. They had decided to just have a break, as tomorrow they would spend the entire day planning when and how to ambush or attack King William. First, they decided to have a snowball fight, it was Winter after all! The Legends had split themselves up for the game. Lily, Zilas, Estella and Ava were on one team, Alex, Twylar and Moon on the other.

Ava's team had named themselves 'Royalty' and Twylar's team had decided on the name 'The Ducks'. Camilla was outside too, but she was referee. "RIGHT, I WANT A NICE FAIR GAME! START!!" she yelled, as she blew her whistle. "BUT FIRST, MAKE A SNOW CASTLE OR SOMETHING FOR PROTECTION!! WHICHEVER TEAM'S CASTLE GETS KNOCKED DOWN FIRST LOSES!!" announced Camilla, as she sneakily winked at Twylar with her serpent-green eyes. The Ducks had already made themselves a pretty roomy snow castle, with no roof of course! They had some boxes as the staircase leading up to the open roof, so they could fire snowballs from the safety of their own castle.

"BEGIN!" yelled Camilla, as soon as she saw team Royalty's castle already built. But unluckily for them, The Ducks had already thought of a gameplan. "alright, so Moon, because of your amazing meteor and animal powers, you're on guard. Make sure no one gets past you unless its us!" Twylar pointed to herself and Alex, Moon just nodded. "Alex, since you can make yourself levitate, I feel like it's best you should be throwing the snowballs, since you could throw some with your hands and multiple using your power!" she continued, Alex also nodded. "and I'll try to sabotage team Royalty.. wait I can just pause time-" Twylar realised, but it seemed like Camilla had also realised that. "BY THE WAY TWYLAR, YOU CAN'T USE YOUR DARK AMETHYST FORM! STICK TO BEING A LIGHT AMETHYST!" she yelled.

Twylar groaned miserably, and yelled back "OKK!!" but then, her face lit up. "wait I have my yellow flames.. I can just melt their castle!!" she smirked. Meanwhile, with team Royalty, they were also thinking of a plan. "Zilas, use your barrier powers to protect this castle, I can cut all the snowballs they hurl at us and Estella, try to invade The Ducks' castle using your invisibility." Commanded Ava. They all nodded. "alright, I'll sneak in now, Moon make sure to be on guard, and Alex start collecting!" whispered Twylar, as she sneaked out through the emergency exit they had made at the back.

Her healing powers were useless right now, and if she used her flames it would gather their attention, so how was she supposed to sneak in? Luckily, Alex managed to levitate her, she floated near the open roof of team Royalty's castle, she could see them down below, whispering to each other in hushed voices. But where was Estella? It was only then that Twylar realised she must be trying to sneak into their castle, she looked back and could see Moon, with two bears at her side. They immediately sniffed out poor Estella, and dragged her away from The Ducks' snow castle. Alex's powers were fading away, and Twylar could feel herself gently dropping down. Alex was now collecting and making snowballs, Moon had convinced a few other bears to do the same!

To her horror, Ava had realised that Twylar was hanging a few inches from her head. "GET THE CAGE ESTELLA!!" yelled Ava, as she grabbed onto Twylar. "HEY!!! LET GO!!" screamed Twylar, as Ava tied her up with some rope. Estella had come back, but as she was still invisible, the cage she was holding looked like it was floating in mid-air. Estella revealed herself, and her facial expression confirmed that she didn't like the idea of having a hostage.

Ava commanded Twylar to get in, so, reluctantly she did. Twylar made sure to groan and whine in hopes that maybe if she was too annoying, they would let her go. She kicked at the iron bars which contained her, and screamed relentlessly like a spoiled toddler, all to no avail. "ZILAS! THE BARRIER!" commanded Ava, as she took of a piece of cloth hanging from one of the snow walls. Hidden underneath it, was a lever. She pulled on it, and suddenly a whole castle appeared in front of Twylar. It was like about the size of a normal, average family home, but for the size of a snow castle it was humongous. "WHEN DID YOU HAVE TIME TO BUILD THIS??" shrieked Twylar, she stopped kicking at the bars. "I didn't. some guy in the mall did, he installed it yesterday. When you guys we're asleep. It's not real snow either, it's hard ice." Said Ava, as she knocked on one of the walls. There was a window in the room Twylar was imprisoned at, but she could see a faint, white barrier surrounding the 'snow castle' she could also see the bewildered faces of Moon and Alex. "ok quit tryna destroy their castle.. let's focus on protecting ours first" remarked Alex, as the snowball he had in his hand dropped, so did his jaw. Moon couldn't speak, so she nodded instead. She commanded not only bears but wolves, tigers, horses, whatever seemed to roam the dangerous forests of Bunny Town came to Moon's aid, they guarded all sides and corners of their castle, and Alex stood there, whimpering and cowering at the size of team Royalty's castle. After Camilla confirmed that this was fair, the actual 'snow' war started. All the residents of Bunny Town came to watch, betting on who would win. "great.. The Ducks' are on the defensive.. what d'we do?" asked Zilas, nervously. "we wait." Said Ava, calmly. There was a strange fire in her eyes, a fire of courage. That was what Twylar admired about her best friend. Realising that they had left her unattended, she took the chance to try to burn through her rope. Which, in the end, she managed to do.

After she was free from the ropes that bound her, she tried to burn through the bars, but nothing would work. Suddenly.. that same shrill voice.. "Camilla?" thought Twylar desperately. "yeah, yeah.. you can use it.. but don't use your time powers, cos that's not fair" whispered Camilla, Twylar could hear her exact words as carefully as though Camilla were right beside her. smiling mischievously, Twylar opened up her portal, her yellow burn mark had returned to black, as the dark tentacles that came from her portal grabbed the key, which was hanging off one of the icy walls. They set Twylar free, she kept quiet and sneaked out the room. suddenly she made a dash for the door, but it was locked. She could hear someone's footsteps coming towards the source of

the noise, without any time to react, Ava had caught her. "where d'you think you're going? GET BACK IN THE CAGE!" roared Ava, as she chased after Twylar. Hoping for the best, Twylar jumped into one of her portals, the origin point of where all the black tentacles had came from. The portal closed as soon as Ava tried to jump in after her, Twylar ended up in some dark, and gloomy place. She could see loads of black tentacles surrounding the area.

Suddenly, another portal showed up. Without a second thought, Twylar jumped into it. She fell flat on her face. As she got up, she wasn't in the dark, gloomy place as she was before. She was back, in the middle of the raging snowball war. "TWYYYY!!!" yelled Alex, as he ran from 2 floating snowballs, realising it was probably Estella holding the snowballs, she hurled some at the invisible figure, and the floating snowballs were no longer there.

She could see Ava's livid face through the white barrier, Zilas was inside too. "alright.. change of plan.." huffed Twylar, as she hurried into their sad little castle. "if someone could just.. I don't know, uhm make Zilas lose focus, I could use my yellow flames on their ice castle, we might be able to win." Whispered Twylar hurriedly, as she could hear the snowballs having impact with their animal guards. "I think.. if I distract them pretending like I'm gonna burn something, Moon, maybe you could destroy their castle with your Meteors?" suggested Twylar, as she took a look outside. Their snowball war had gained a huge amount of eager bunnies, betting on who would win and eagerly munching on their carrots. "yeah, that could work!" agreed Alex, in the end, Moon agreed too.

So, Twylar went outside the comfort of her shabby little snow castle, she marched up to the faint, white barrier, her palm was engulfed with her yellow flames but she couldn't feel any pain, her Burn mark had turned yellow, her left eye yellow too, her right eye white. "uhm.. can she burn through my barrier?" asked Zilas, worriedly. He rushed out their ice castle, and tried to refocus so he could make the barrier stronger, but Twylar pretended as though she's received a letter that she could burn through anything, which made Zilas even more anxious. Losing focus, the faint white barrier weakened, allowing Twylar to at least manage to push her fingers through, but not her whole body.

Zilas, getting more worried their plan would fail, lost focus and let go of the barrier completely. "NOW MOON!!" yelled Twylar, as she ran away from the ice castle. Without delay, Moon had summoned a massive meteor, which fell from the sky and landed perfectly on top the ice castle. Zilas, Estella and Ava had made it out unharmed, but what about Lily? "uhm.. did I miss anything?" Lily asked, suspiciously. "okay.. I went to the toilet for 2 minutes and y'all do this?" she said, amazed. Camilla cut through the argument, as she revealed the winner. "SURPRISINGLY, THE DUCKS HAVE WON!!!" she screamed, she ran up to Twylar and gave her a huge hug, which soon Twylar and the rest of the winners were surrounded by flocks of bunnies, asking them random questions and overloading them with a lot more questions on the go. The losers, however, sulked in the corner miserably.

After the swarm of bunnies had finally left the winners alone, they decided to go check on team Royalty. "well that was fun! Wasn't it?" said Moon, trying to lighten up the mood. "for you, maybe.." murmured Zilas. "well, to be honest, that was a good game!" admitted Estella. Soon, there were no more sulking and no more arguments, they all came back together to become 'The Legends' once more. They had spent 20 minutes of their day out with the snowball war, and 5 minutes changing into new clothes and getting rid of dirty, melted snow from their hair. (snow has dirty bacteria in it, which means it's bad for your health if you drink melted snow water. Search it up)

After that, The Legends decided to visit the beach, for what seemed like the 5th time. Once they arrived, they rushed to the changing rooms to change into swimwear, but Ava, Moon and Twylar wore t-shirts. "it ain't my fault that Bunny Town doesn't sell human-sized clothes!!" murmured Twylar. "well to be fair I got all of my clothes from Dragon Thorn, but my dad says now that they're in an alliance with The Isle Of Irene, he won't let me shop there.. mainly because we're wanted.." interrupted Estella, as she came out her changing room. Once all of them got changed, they rushed (all of them raced towards the sea- Ava won the race) towards the sea, suddenly, Lily had a mischievous thought. She dived under the water, and stayed there. Waiting. Waiting. For what seemed like hours, but was actually minutes, she still hadn't come back up. The Legends were starting to get worried, but not Alex. "she's gonna splash us, isn't she.." he whispered, nervously to Twylar "obviously.. let's take cover before she can splash us.." murmured Twylar. Hurriedly, the two brainstormed ideas of where to hide, and realised they could search by air. "Twylar decided to watch Lily torment The Legends from a high cliff, she was sure Lily wouldn't notice her up there. Alex, soon after, decided to join her.

They waited. And after 5 minutes of continued calling and shouts for Lily, she emerged (as expected) from the sea. She was a giant siren, of course. The ocean's heart lay sunken deep beneath the skin of her forehead, it was glowing in rhythm. Like a heartbeat. And, as expected, she mercilessly showered everyone with waterfalls of salty, sea-water. Everyone got their fair share, before Estella decided to turn invisible, climb up Lily's back and sneakily guided Moon to do the same. Surprisingly, the shark Moon was carrying up Lily's back did not move, only until it was placed upon Lily's messy, jungle-like dark hair, that it started ripping out handfuls of it with its mouth.

Zilas, however, managed to get at least a little wet, as he proved that his barrier power was a useful ability. Twylar found that Alex couldn't take his eyes off Estella. She nudged him gently at first, but he didn't respond. So, Twylar took matters into her own hands. She concentrated for a second, and paused time. It was still weird and freaky to her, that when she tried to feel for her normal human ears they weren't there, instead it was like they were never there at all! All she got for ears were Black wolf-like ears at the top of her head, it blended in with her hair. Meaning half of it was white. (only the tips, though)

She scrambled to reach Estella, she found her soaking wet because of Lily, but she was playfully chasing after Moon. She was in the motion of running, the sand was falling out her hands and onto the ground. Slowly but carefully, Twylar led Estella up to the cliff Alex was at, (getting Estella up the cliff was tricky, but she transformed into a wolf and flew up it with Estella on her back.)

Once Estella was finally up the cliff, Twylar un-paused time. "what am I-" she began. Alex threw Twylar a deadly look. "uh h-hi Estella.." he mumbled, he just managed to edge away from her. "hm? You sound sick? Are you sure your alright?" she asked, her voice full of care for her friend. "ha-ha.." he let out the fakest laugh ever. "are you sure Alex?" she insisted. "it's nice to have that one friend who's just too good for you.." Twylar whispered, she made sure Alex had heard her. "Twy? Did you say something?" asked Estella. "heh no, I was just coughing.. it's kinda cold here, don't you think?" answered Twylar.

Estella smiled at them both warmly "alright, if it ever gets too cold you two can head back to the castle. I'll tell the others- not now of course, you haven't told me if you want to go back!" she said, and with that she headed off, she climbed back down, not questioning how she managed to get up there in the first place. Alex stared at her longingly, as she climbed all the way down back to a very confused Ava. "AAAHHHH I HATE YOU TWYYY" he blurted out, as soon as Estella was distracted by Ava. "I mean.. I had to do something I ain't sitting here watching ma bestie get tortured by love" she teased, Twylar added a lot of emphasis on the 'love' bit.

Alex curled himself up, and covered his face. His dark, curly purple hair all over the place- "I guess everyone's dying their hair nowadays.. wait no Alex's hair is natural.." thought Twylar, as she thought of Ava's light blue, DYED hair. Soon, night fell and The Legends were huddled together on the sand, watching the sunset. Soon after the moon rose, and they headed back to the castle. (they changed back into their normal clothes first)

Once they were back at the castle, Lily found her room yet again overcrowded by The Legends, they just chatted and surprisingly, no one brought up the topic of the spirit forest. "oh my gosh.." remembered Twylar, as she put down her strawberry boba. "sorry I just remembered something.." she apologised. "no, go on!" insisted Estella. Zilas looked around for his red bandana, and clumsily put it on "yeah, go on?" he blurted out. "basically.." began Twylar. A memory flashed before her eyes as she told the story of that day...

It was in year 6. The last year of primary school. Willow, Ava, Moon and Lily were walking to school together earlier that morning, accompanied by a royal guard. Christie, Sammy and Stacey were already in class, and they were late. "sorry 'bout this, Mrs Clark it's the demon's fault." Said the royal guard. The teacher, whose name was Mrs Clark, nodded, and sternly looked at Twylar. A look of pure disgust. "it's actually my fault miss, I forgot my bag and I made them wait for me" admitted Ava "mine too! I convinced them to hang around at the park for a while!" lied Willow. Her brown skin was soft and smooth, her eyelashes were long and her hair braided and tied.

Mrs Clark sternly looked at all of them, giving Twylar the longest death stare imaginable. "oh yeah, mine too I uhm.. I also forgot my bag!" lied Moon. "alright, ALRIGHT!" yelled Mrs Clark. "you five will get detention with me after school." She decided. All of them sat in their seats and waited for break. "thanks guys.." mumbled Twylar, as she noticed 'the troublesome trio' coming towards them. "what d'you want Christie?" said Ava, standing in front of Twylar. "haha! I thought an elite like you would at least tell the difference between friend or- in this case, demon!" snorted Christie.

Willow rolled her eyes. "Yeah, Twylar's definitely a demon!" agreed Stacey. "Ugh, will you ever shut up? Can we enjoy our 5 minute break?" said Willow, annoyed. "Hah! With her, you can't," said Stacey, as she pointed towards Twylar. "OI EVERYONE! TWYLAR'S A DEMON!!" yelled Christie. All eyes were on Twylar now. "DEMON! DEMON! DEMON!" the crowd chanted. Twylar stood in the middle of the crowd, breathing heavily and glancing over at every eye staring her way. She looked from one person to the next. She could see the girls whispering, the boys pointing and laughing- "I think that's called 'social anxiety' but I'm not sure", interrupted Estella. Twylar paused with her story, and turned to check the time. "Woah it's already past midnight.. well, goodnight guys!" said Twylar, as she leapt up from her chair and rushed to her comfy, soft bed. "Sweet bliss!" she sighed, as she sank deep into the red, floral patterned cover.

Chapter Four

The next day, The Legends woke up extra early, ate their breakfast (which was made by Moon; Estella handed out the orange juice), and headed to the meeting room. There, they found the chief commander of the bunny army. There was a menacing scar covering his eye! There was also the Bunny King, The Legends never got to know his actual name. (even though Estella had told them a million times!) Camilla was also there; she and Twylar had not spoken for a few days.

Camilla smiled, and The Legends sat down. "Ok, so I was thinking The Legends should go sneak into the forest, avoid any spirit we come across, and protect the border of the forest from King William." Suggested Moon. "Yeah, we should take some guards with us! If dad would let us…?" said Estella, who was sitting next to the Bunny King. The king just smiled and nodded. After one hour of discussing plans, they decided to stick with Moon's plan.

After they finished the meeting, they headed outside. They saw the familiar landscape of the castle fields; they could see the place where they had their snowball war a couple of minutes away! Right now, they were standing in the spot where they had been at that tug-of-war game. "Y'know, it's kinda sad…" said Moon, as she looked around one last time. "Yeah, after like two weeks, this place is like our home!" agreed Twylar. "Wait, you've been here for two weeks!?" gasped Zilas. "It's literally just two weeks, Z…" murmured Ava. "Alright. Camilla stays in the castle, uhm.." began Twylar before catching Camilla's eye. She was smiling, but her eyes indicated that she was feeling lonely. Makes sense, though; she's been left out whenever The Legends go on an 'adventure.

They made half of the journey by car, but since it was so small only two people managed to fit inside. Twylar was with Alex, Ava, and Zilas were in one car, too. Estella, Moon and Lily had managed to squeeze themselves into a single car. The one-hour-long journey began, and Lily soon began wishing she hadn't squished herself to sit next to Moon and

Estella. Alex and Twylar were a bit chatty, so they ended up annoying their poor taxi driver. "Also, how's it going with Estella?" asked Twylar cheekily. "Meh... it's fine!" Alex replied. He stared absent-mindedly out the window. "You're so in love..." sighed Twylar. "I-I'm not! It's just I kinda don't wanna ruin our friendship," he admitted. Twylar listened; she stared at Alex with confusion in her eyes. "Well, what am I supposed to do when Estella actually likes me too?" he reasoned. "I kinda just like being her friend, even though I do have a crush on her. It's just because she's a really nice person, and I wanna spend more time with her," he began. "Basically, whenever a guy thinks he has a crush, it's actually just them really wanting to be around the person they like, and they REALLY like that person, but the guy misinterpreted it as love", he explained. "And, like, what would actually happen if your crush liked you back? What are you supposed to do then? And what if this is like in year 4 or something? What are you supposed to do!? You definitely can't date as kids." He paused for a second. "Plus, I really like Estella, but it's not the love kind of like. I do have a crush on her, but it's not the love type of crush. Do you get me?" he asked. Twylar bluntly shook her head. "I mean, I get what you're saying, but not the last part" she said, as she stared out the small, carrot-shaped window. She could see the world go by.

She could see a bunny walking a dog. Which seems weird as they're both animals... totally logical. Just an average day in Bunny Town. "Yeah, I guess you're right. Crushes aren't actually what you might think they are sometimes. Also, I know for sure I ain't dating some love-sick guy... I'M A CONFIDENT INDEPENDENT WOMAN!!" she yelled, suddenly realising how their taxi driver wasn't saying anything. "Yeah, the world's full of arguments and almost all of them are caused because of couples. There are breakups and cheaters everywhere... which is also why I'm not really interested in dating anyone," said Alex as he got out of the car. They had made it to their destination: just the Bunny Town harbour. They were the first to arrive, so they waited the next hour for everyone else.

Once all The Legends were there, they headed east. Lily picked all of them up in siren form; all she had to do was just walk a couple of steps, and they'd arrived. The Spirit Forest was covered in autumn leaves. The trees had almost all their leaves fallen off. Only the yellow leaves remained. Nervously, they all entered. Almost immediately, a cold gush of wind tinkled through their bodies, but they pushed forward. The ground was nice and clean, except it was littered with branches and sticks; orange, yellow and red leaves surrounded every path The Legends took, and the air smelled fresh and crisp. Suddenly, two girls approached them. "Spirits!" yelled Ava as she pulled out her sword. "Don't worry, travellers, we're just curious! No one's ever come to visit us," said the blonde girl. The other girl behind her had messy, red hair. "My name's Celestial, and this is my sister, Rose." She explained. The red-haired girl, whose name was Rose, smiled and waved.

She took a step forward. "We have two other sisters, Winter and Summer. Ma didn't give them normal human names, favouritism...," said Rose. Darkly. "Oh, and by the way, Rose is the spirit of Autumn, and I'm the spirit of Spring!" interrupted Celestial as she peered at the first-ever humans to come into The Spirit Forest. Alive. Twylar looked at them questioningly. Celestial's blonde hair reminded her of Queen Amber's. She had elf-like ears and freckles and brown eyes full of curiosity. She had a flower crown placed on top of her head, and she wore one big pink rose as her shirt and nothing else. Her skirt was just left!

As for Rose, she too had elf-like ears, her messy red hair reached her legs, and she had fiery orange eyes. And, just like her sister, she also had freckles. Rose was wearing a dress made out of fallen autumn leaves; the leaves that covered her body were orange, and both sisters were barefoot. "Uhm... so, we're protecting you guys against Willow and King William..." began Alex. "Willow? I think I've heard that name before... come with us!" said Celestial cheerily. "Well... they seem friendly?" said Twylar. She shrugged and ran after them. Soon followed by the rest of The Legends. They stopped, and they found themselves in a village. There were spirits left and right, and Celestial hurried The Legends inside a house. "Celestial, are these the humans asking about Willow?" asked another girl, this time with light blue hair. Twylar looked closely, and she could see the blue-haired girl also had icy blue eyes. There was a snowflake clip on her head, and her dress was white. She had small, see-through wings. Almost as if they were made out of ice.

The other girl had brown hair; she seemed warm and friendly, just like Celestial; her brown hair reached up to her legs, the same as the blue-haired girl. "Oh, this is Summer and Winter! I'm sure you can guess what spirits they are!" giggled Celestial. "Listen, human, the reason your kind never leave this forest is because we weigh their hearts. We see their good and bad. If they are good, they are allowed to leave. If they are bad, the spirit of fire deals with them," said Winter as she jabbed her finger at Zilas.

"Sister, don't scare them! I can tell that they have good hearts." Said Summer. "Oh, and Celestial, bring back spring because I've taken down Winter. Rose, let Celestial bring Spring to our forest, too." Interrupted Winter. Rose groaned, and suddenly, all the tree's leaves were back, the grass was no longer littered with fallen leaves, and flowers were to be seen everywhere. "So... is this how we have four seasons?" asked Alex. "Oh no, we could never do that! We are spirits, not gods. It is he who has blessed us with this power." Explained Summer. All the spirits were not as you would expect. They were the size of a normal human and not like the elves and fairies in those children's books. "Well, we know the name of Willow but not much about her. For that, you need to see our chief. If you're with us, you will be safe. If we get separated, just stay away from Eris. She is the spirit of discord. You can probably tell because she took some Greek goddess name." Said Summer, she took Twylar's hand in hers. "I know we can expect great things from you; that burn mark is no ordinary mark", she continued.

Alex stared uncomfortably out the window. Twylar could tell he was getting anxious. "Alright, let's go see the chief... there are some things we need to tell him- "began Twylar, "it's a she", interrupted Winter. So, they set off. Celestial was cheery all throughout the journey, Winter seemed distant and cold, Summer didn't say much, and Rose was very grumpy. "Why're you so grumpy?" asked Celestial as she walked side-by-side with Rose. "Because... it's Spring now, and I feel like Autumn looked way better!" groaned Rose. They had managed to reach halfway in one day, so they slept in the woods. The spirits, who had known the spirit forest all their lives, slept peacefully on the soft, green grass.

The Legends came up with loads of wild ideas to stay off the ground! Alex tried levitating himself and slept in the air. Moon crept away from the little green patch of earth they were supposed to sleep on, somehow found the spirit of animals and convinced him to give Moon one of his bears, so Moon slept peacefully on the bear's fluffy, brown stomach. Lily decided to just deal with it and slept on the ground along with the other spirits, but soon after seeing one huge spider attempting to crawl up her leg, Lily decided she would not even look at the grass anymore. So, she found herself sleeping on top of the bear's back. Now, the poor creature was being used as a bed, as Ava and Estella had crawled next to the bear's back and slept soundly, but Estella found there was no more room on the bear for her to sleep on. Zilas used his barrier to ensure that he was not touching the grass, and Twylar lay high up on a tree, curled up in between the branches. Alex was also near her too, he was staring anxiously down below.

Twylar looked down; she couldn't see anything. "Alex, what're you staring at?" whispered Twylar. "Oh uh... just thought I saw a shadow..." he mumbled as he turned over. "Ouch... that looks uncomfortable..." thought Twylar as she stared at her best friend, who was floating in the air, birds surrounding him, and the cold slicing against his cheek. Twylar stared down again; this time, she could see the shadow of someone with very long hair and horns at the top of their head; their elf-like ears and what seemed like a lizard tail followed them behind. The shadow's appearance just screamed "Eris..." thought Twylar darkly. She closed her eyes and tried her hardest to sleep.

She drifted off to her own dreamworld, and this time, she could see the warm smile of her mother, her beautiful blonde hair, those sparkling eyes... Queen Amber. Suddenly, she held her arms forward, ready to embrace Twylar in her arms; she leaned forward. Suddenly, the image of Twylar's mother disappeared, and Twylar could see the destruction of The Isle of Irene. It was the same nightmare. Over and over again. But no, instead of King William standing on top of that balcony, it was Twylar. The War. Everything up until now had seemed like a daydream. The Legends had to win the war. They had Bunny Town on their side. Now, they needed to win over the chief of spirits. Twylar awoke and was back on her tree. She had woken up early, because right now the sun was rising. Twylar could see the sun steadily rising. It reminded her how fast days go by and how fast this great war would come. The Legends are up against The Isle of Irene. Turns out she wasn't the only one awake too. "Hey Twylar! Wanna help me cook breakfast?" called Celestial. Twylar looked down and saw Summer and Celestial huddled around an open fire. "Right, we making eggs?" asked Twylar as she hopped down from her tree. "Yeah, Rose is getting some fish- she found a river near us", said Summer as she turned over the eggs. "And Winter is still sleeping, but the smell will probably wake her up." Said Celestial, as she prepared some leaf plates and some branches, which were supposed to be the knife and fork. The bear was sleeping, Estella and Ava were on its back, Moon on its stomach and Lily on its back. Zilas woke up; he looked around and saw that breakfast was almost ready.

With a yawn, he put down his barrier and stepped out. "Morning..." he said sleepily. "Oh yeah, uh, could you go wake up the others?" asked Twylar as she added a bit of seasoning to the egg. Zilas groaned to show how unhappy he was and jabbed the bear in the face. It roared angrily and sped off towards the trees. Everyone who was sleeping on the bear woke up and sat next to Twylar. They had their eyes closed whilst they were sitting cross-legged. Soon, Winter woke up. "Seriously... he's still up there?" questioned Ava as she saw Alex floating up in the air. "Hey, uh... Moon? Could you, like, I don't know, summon a meteor just next to Alex so he wakes up?" suggested Ava as she was handed her leaf plate. Moon nodded as she nearly gave Alex a heart attack. He came tumbling down and crashed into a bush. "Morning..." he moaned. His purple hair was all over the place. There were twigs and leaves on it, too.

After plucking out all the leaves from his hair, he joined the rest of The Legends. "Mmm", sighed Estella as she ate her eggs and fish. "Anyone want more eggs? I have three extra?" asked Summer. "MEEEE!!!" shouted Lily instantly. Lily was handed all three of the eggs, and she munched greedily on all her food. Once they finished their breakfast, they continued on their journey. They had reached what seemed like an abnormally large tree though all the trees in the spirit forest were tall, this one was the tallest. They were engulfed in the shadows of the leaves. It was like the blue sky had turned green! "This is it!" said Summer, cheerily. "Right... come on in Twyl-"began Celestial as she took a step towards the huge tree.

Winter stopped her sister. "You're underage; they'll have to come with Summer and me." She said, with a voice as cold as ice. "Sorry! Rose ran off again... gotta find where she went! Celestial, help me find her!" asked Summer as she led Celestial off into the woods. "Alright... stay back." Commanded Winter. "She gives me the chills..." murmured Zilas. "Same here, Z.." agreed Ava, rubbing her hands for warmth. "Don't be dramatic, she's literally the spirit of Winter, stupid!" said Moon as she rolled her eyes. "I'm not stu-"began Zilas before pausing and jabbing his finger at Winter. She had opened up a sort of rabbit hole in the tree, and then, she jumped down it. Ava reluctantly followed. Moon and Lily hugged each other as they tumbled down. Estella simply let herself fall, and soon, Alex and Twylar were the only ones. "Wait... are we gonna end up in Wonderland or something?" commented Twylar as she peered down the hole in the massive tree.

Alex peered down, too and gulped. "Wait... are we really trusting someone who acts like they don't even know what kindness is?" asked Alex nervously. "Well... risk it for the biscuit! GERONIMOOO!!!" shouted Twylar as she curled herself into a tight ball and tumbled down the rabbit hole. "Ok, one... there is no biscuit, two GERONOMO'S AN AMERICAN SAYING!! WE'RE IN THE SPIRIT FORESTTT!!" yelled Alex, hoping that Twylar would hear him from down there. Suddenly, he saw that shadow again. Eris. He gulped and jumped down the hole. He landed with a splat on the floor, but he wasn't hurt. "Took you long enough!" exclaimed Lily as she stared at her surroundings. "LILY MY GIRL... I THOUGHT WE WOULD'T MAKE ITTT!!!" screamed Moon from behind as she suddenly hug-attacked Lily.

Alex stared around, too, and saw Estella; his heart took a backflip. But then, he remembered Estella was nice and all, but he didn't want to ruin their friendship! He has no keen eye on them actually getting together, so technically, it's not love. Just admiring someone because they're really cool? Yeah, that seems to be the case. He stared up at the rabbit hole he dropped down from; now, there was no hole. Twylar dusted herself off; the inside of the great tree was what you'd expect of a large, comfy wooden treehouse. Lanterns lit with golden crackling fire hung at every corner of the room, vines creeping up the wooden walls, and even a fireplace was there, adding to the comfiness. There were about 3 doors, two on either side of the fireplace and the other behind them. Winter checked if everyone was there and strode off towards the left side of the fireplace.

The next room had wooden walls with the same vines, but there was red carpet along the floor, leading to a wooden ladder. "Alright, this ladder leads to the top of this tree, but of course, spirits have faster methods of travel." Snorted Winter. She swiftly pulled out what seemed like a brown bag, pulled out a handful of stuff, and whispered something into it. "These are jade seeds. You know one of the Crystal Wolf species, the Jade Wolf? Yeah, they make these," said Winter as she showed everyone the bag. "We're in 2025... already invented ways of teleportation... yayy" said Alex, sarcastically, as he put out a thumbs up. "It's December, soon it'll be 2026. I bet everyone will get powers like royalty, even out in the real world," commented Twylar. "Alright, everyone, hold onto me!" commanded Winter.

They did as they were told, Winter whispered into the jade seeds, and suddenly, Twylar felt as if she was about to faint. She could tell everyone felt the same way, all around her was blurry. It looked as though they were spinning! Winter, however, had no reaction. Her light blue hair simply blew in the 'light breeze'; meanwhile, Twylar was getting attacked by what felt like a tornado. She wished she had just flown all the way up the stairs. When they finally reached the top of the tree, they found themselves in an open room, there were no walls and all there was to stand on was just a wooden floor. There was a red carpet, a hole where the ladder was, and a golden throne. Sitting on that golden throne was the chief of spirits. "Chief, humans... they wanted to speak with you," announced Winter. "Ah, dear, I told you to call me Paris! That goes for you humans, too." Said the chief; she had freckles, and like Celestial, she had golden hair. Her elf-like ears stuck out, and she was barefoot like all the spirits The Legends had met.

She smiled at them and beckoned for them to come closer. "Oh? This one's not a human... a werewolf! Oh? And these four are nillaphards?" questioned Paris. "Oh my... yes, yes... you are destined for great things, Twylar... and you must do it alone..." said Paris in a distant voice. "But... I can't do it alone, miss," answered Twylar. "But then again... the future can change even by the slightest thing; just know that no one can tell you what your future is going to be. Only you can decide that." Whispered Paris, she pointed a finger at Twylar. "And you, the nillaphards, how have you been granted this power? Every nillaphard has a story to tell." She said, facing Moon, Lily and Ava. "Uhm... by Queen Amber?" said Moon, not sure if it was the right answer.

Paris smiled and opened her mouth to speak. "Ah, yes! Queen Amber! She was a good friend of mine, light amethyst, am I correct?" Suddenly, she was facing Twylar now. Twylar nodded. "Uh... yeah, uhm, King William's planning on taking spirit souls so that he can like... yeah, I'm not going into details..." shivered Twylar. "Right, right... don't worry. I have sent every spirit willing to defend us to the shores, led by Eris." Answered Paris. "Oh, and... do you know where Willow is?" asked Ava. "Ah, yes! Willow, Willow... is she the nillaphard with the weather powers?" asked Paris. "Yeah, and what's a nillaphard?" asked Alex. "Oh right, it's an elf saying... it means someone who was born without powers but grew up to have one, like you four." Answered Paris, pointing at Ava, Moon and Lily.

"But... aren't I a nillaphard?" questioned Twylar. "No, see, you already had Crystal Wolf blood running through your veins; your mother's soul inside you is what makes you half-light amethyst. You are very unique,

Twylar. There is no other like you in the whole world!" complimented Paris. "Anyways... about Willow, I'm afraid there is a long way to go to reach her... are you willing to rescue her?" said Paris, facing all of The Legends. "The place where she is kept cannot be broken into. Even my most powerful spirits cannot break in." Paris continued, "Here, take this map. I fear you may meet Drew; he is the spirit of wild beasts." She warned. And

with that, The Legends followed the map all the way down the tree, off to the coast of the river flamingo. "Why were we sent on this dragon quest?" straight out of a game, I say!" commented Lily. "Lil McGee, my dearest friend, we have to save Willow like she's somewhere here! Just really, REALLY far away..." said Twylar as she stepped closer to the bank. She peered deep into the murky waters of the river flamingo. Long ago, it was said to be home to the most exotic flamingos, even the rare white swan. That's what they called it though, 'Koshi' was its actual species name. White flamingos. The rarest animal in the world. "Ugh, where are the Koshis??" groaned Lily as she stared around. "No idiot, Koshis are the prey of crocodile

es. Who lives here, dummy!" snorted Ava as she took a step closer. Twylar put her hand in the water, and Ava was next to her, peering into the salty water. "CROCODILES!??" screamed Zilas as he ran as far as he could from the river. "Z, crocodiles aren't even scary like- "began Twylar before catching a glimpse of bumpy, green skin.

She instantly stepped back, "CROCODILESSSS!!!!" she screamed, running to catch up with Zilas. "HIYAH!" shouted Zilas as he threw his red bandana. It didn't even touch the crocodile. It landed pathetically on the grass. The crocodile emerged from the river it headed towards Alex, before Moon used her power on it to coax it back to the river. "Yeah... uh, Lil, could you transform and carry us across?" asked Moon as she checked if the crocodile was gone. "Yeah..." replied Lily, as she quickly dived into the water and re-emerged as a siren. She carried Alex, Zilas and Estella across first before returning to carry Twylar, Ava and Moon.

Once they made it over the river flamingo, they carried on their journey by air. By doing this, they avoided a lot of obstacles, which would've cost them more precious time! Moon was being carried by a very large bird. Lily transformed into a Siren with legs and carried Ava, Estella and Zilas. Alex just drifted off, as he had levitated himself, and Twylar flew as a wolf. "It's been three months, and I'm still not getting used to this..."

thought Twylar wearily as she stared at her black fur. They made it halfway when they noticed something down below, a spirit. He was sitting by a tree quietly reading a book while what looked like a purple dragon ran around in circles playfully. Getting curious, Twylar flew down to meet this stranger. Followed unwillingly by the rest of The Legends, they all flew down (except for Lily first; she put everyone she was carrying down, and then she transformed)

He was so lost in the book he was reading that the spirit didn't even notice the humans coming towards him. Suddenly, the purple dragon hissed at them and alerted its owner. "Oh! Uhm... Kiara, don't attack!" commanded the spirit, and the purple dragon, whose name was Kiara, sat down reluctantly. "Uhm, did Paris send you? In that case, I'm Drew" he stumbled up and put down his book. On closer inspection, he was wearing glasses and had curly brown hair. His elf ears stuck out, and his eyes were green.

"Drew!?" wondered Zilas, suddenly feeling suspicious. "Oh, uh, meet Kiara! She's an uh... a dragon," he stammered. Kiara spat out fire angrily. "Oh, uh... Drew? You know what? I think we'd best be on our way..." suggested Ava, "no, I get that... everyone takes one look at me and decides to just go... thanks for even talking, I guess..." he said miserably. "No! Wait up!" interrupted Twylar as he began to walk off. Drew turned around, "Hehe.. one reason why no one wants to be friends with me is cos of... PFFT HAHAHAHA" he laughed. He reminded Twylar of Christie... the same psychopathic laugh... "HAHA- I can't... you seriously fell for that?" he joked. "KIARA! NOW!" he yelled, and all he did then was just step back. "WHY COULDN'T SUMMER AND WINTER COME WITH US!!" screamed Alex as he cowered behind Ava. Kiara, the big purple dragon, smiled mischievously and puffed out a bit of smoke. "Phew..." sighed Twylar. But Kiara had roared out the blazing fire this time. "TWYY MAYBE YOU SHOULDN'T TRUST STRANGERS THAT MUCH!??" yelled Alex. He stood behind Estella, both of them bearing swords. "Where'd you find those?" asked Ava, turning around, "near this tree," replied Estella, as she pointed at a tree near her.

Ava turned around to face Kiara. "How convenient..." she wondered. She was bearing her sword, which could cut through anything. She knew that to ensure that her friends were safe, she needed to dash in and end it all. "TWY! DESTRACT KIARA," yelled Ava, and Twylar did exactly that.

As quick as lightning, Ava swooped in and charged. They left the battleground with Drew tied to a tree and Kiara slain. "Wow... who knew this was going to be some dragon-slaying quest?" said Lily sarcastically. They spent all of their evening travelling to the place where Willow was kept. The map did lead them off course, but it turns out it was just a shortcut from incoming danger. They had made it to the place Willow was kept. They found her tied up on a tree, surrounded by spirits.

One spirit gave her a bowl of water, and Willow slurped it up thirstily. "HELP!!" she cried, realising The Legends were there. And help they did. Moon just summoned a meteor to land straight on the spirits, and they had some difficulty untying the rope, but Ava cut it off. "WILLOW!!" shouted Twylar as she squeezed her tightly. "Heh... take it easy, Twy!" she laughed. "How did you know I was here?" she asked. "To be honest, the bunny agents did it all for us", admitted Moon. "So, you got the bunny army?" said Willow, with a mixed expression of sadness and disappointment in her eyes. "Yeah, we did! Let's go back to Bunny Town," suggested Twylar as she gestured for Lily to transform. They travelled all the way back to the tall tree and met up with Winter. "So, you succeeded?"

 Guessed Winter as she led them to Paris. "Yeah," confirmed Lily. Willow sulked. Soon, when she had a chance to properly speak with The Legends alone, she spoke, "Uhm... are we still going to do this, war?" Willow asked. "Of course! We need to save everyone from King Willia-"began Twylar. "No, Twy, I don't think we can be friends... and I mean that for all The Legends- and whoever that guy is", said Willow, firmly, as she pointed at Zilas. "B-but Willow-"stammered Twylar. "No! I just don't wanna get hurt in the war... I'm going to live in Volcano Hills with my Ma, and don't think I'm coming back!" snorted Willow, "and I'll make use of these weather powers-"she began when she attempted to use her power, she found she suddenly can't. She tried again and again to use it, but she just couldn't.

Twylar, with tears in her eyes, stepped back and let Ava argue with Willow. Whilst she was doing that, Lily and Moon ran to comfort her, like the day they found out Queen Amber was dead. Zilas, Alex and Estella tried to stop Ava from going into total beast mode, all to no avail. The legends knew what had just happened had hurt Twylar the most, for she and Willow had some history with each other. When Willow joined Twylar's school, she was fierce and brave. She became instantly friends with Twylar, and she protected her. Twylar looked up to Willow. They were the best of friends. Until Willow left for Ever Green, but she came back and left again. Winter used the jade seeds on Willow, transporting her to Volcano Hills. There, she made new friends. Mia and Melody. Siblings. She created an entirely different life from the one she used to have, and her family was right there beside her.

Twylar, still heartbroken, travelled to Bunny Town with the help of Winter's miraculous jade seeds. After they reached the bunny castle, Twylar had completely forgotten about Willow. "Come on, let's go tell your dad that we made an alliance with the spirits-"began Ava. "Wait... we did?" questioned Zilas. "Yes, Z, now come, or the King'll think we died", joked Twylar. "But Twy.. you were really upset about Willow..." reasoned Zilas. "I'm trying really hard to forget about it... and you're not helping", she snapped as she swiftly ran into the bunny castle. After everyone had taken a warm shower, eaten and changed into new clothes, they headed to the king's quarters.

Once they arrived, they saw the king tucked up in his bed, his ears flopped down, and he didn't have the energy to even look at his daughter! "Dad?" asked Estella nervously. She sat on her father's bed. He felt for Estella's wavy pink hair and smiled weakly. "Deathbells," he muttered. "Deathbells.. his majesty's got an illness... a very severe one, in fact, no cure", explained the bunny doctor next to him. "Deathbells starts with a tiny ringing in your ear before then getting louder. That ringing signals to the brain that you are in danger of dying, and it makes the brain shut off... right now, his majesty is going through that brain shut-off thing..." said the doctor sadly. Estella, with tears in her eyes, just nodded.

"But.. who's gonna be king now?" whispered Estella as she wiped her tears away. "First my mum.. then the Bunny King.. who next?" thought Twylar darkly, as she listened in to Estella and the doctor's conversation. "Well, princess, I assume it must be you." Announced the doctor. "B-but... I can't! I can't just become Queen of a land, a kingdom of bunnies! No, that would be absurd.." soon Estella began talking to herself out loud. "What a nice, formal vocabulary.." snorted Lily. She received an elbow digging deep into her skin by Moon.

Estella thought for a moment, "Oh! Uh, why couldn't Uncle Ronnie rule?" asked Estella. "Anna" coughed the king, he was silent for a long time. And that was his final word before he drifted off into a nightmarish sleep, one where he would never meet his daughter again unless she, too, had that nightmare. He was dead. "A-Anna? Oh, I'm so stupid.. yes! Anna can be Queen!" suggested Estella, not realising her father was dead. "As in your cousin? Not related by blood?" asked the doctor. "Yes, she's a vegetarian fox, so the bunnies should be safe." Said Estella calmly while she placed her hand on her father's body. "A FOX? A FOX RULLING US?" spat the doctor.

Estella nodded. "She's vegetarian. She thinks of bunnies as normal as she would of other foxes." Said Estella. She stood up suddenly. "His hand... it's cold..." she muttered. The doctor immediately checked the king's pulse, only to find there was none. "AAAAAAAAAAAAAAAAAAAAAAAAHHHHHH" screamed Estella as she dashed out of the room. "HEY!" yelled Alex, running after her. "Let's leave 'em... hehe..." said Moon cheekily. "No, idiot, he said he just wanted to be friends! You weirdo..." remarked Twylar as she dashed after Alex. Once Twylar finally caught up with Alex, he was standing outside Estella's locked bedroom door. "ESTELLA! OPEN UP!" yelled Twylar as she knocked on the door. "Let me talk, Twy," interrupted Alex. Twylar stepped aside and let him do the talking.

Chapter Five

With a heavy heart, Twylar retreated and told Ava everything. She tied her long, light blue hair in a ponytail and stormed upstairs to Estella's room. "AVA!" yelled Moon as she followed after her. Twylar, Zilas and Lily rushed to the king's quarters. They saw the lifeless body of the bunny king, and several new doctors had arrived at the scene. The moon rose, and soon it was nighttime. The trees were stripped of their leaves. Winter was a very scary season. "Just like the spirit herself," thought Twylar as she thought of the fearsome spirit of Winter. Twylar was standing outside, alone, on her balcony. She watched countless birds fly by before settling her eyes on something. A shadow darted across the bushes. Twylar blinked. She blinked again. Nothing was there. "huh..." she thought as she headed inside.

The next day, Estella stood at the top of a stage. Her cousin, Anna, was standing next to her. "Good morning, everyone, I can tell you already know about our king's sudden death... and I am not going to be your queen, but my cousin." Said Estella formally. She looked at her cousin. "This is Anna; she will be your Queen. She is not my cousin by blood, and yes, she is a fox." Announced Estella. "Don't worry! I'm a vegetarian," interrupted Anna, followed by instant sighs of relief. "I am currently travelling with The Legends, and we have made some alliances. We call ourselves the Allies. Yes, we did take the name from World War II, but this is going to be another world war," continued Estella, "and you can probably guess who the Axis are- just another sign that we're gonna win this!" Joked Anna. "Anyways," said Estella, eyeing her cousin. "Bunny Town, Spirit Forest and Ever Green are supporting the Allies, so they will be included in the war. We have received several other letters, but we'll get down to that later." Finished Estella. She placed her silver crown on top of Anna's furry fox head.

Estella rushed to her friends— the roaring cheers of the crowd almost deafened poor Anna, who had spent life as a princess in Volcano Hills.

Once the crowd finally got on with their own lives, Twylar found the chance to speak with Anna. "Uhm.. hi, you're from Volcano Hills, right?" asked Twylar. "Yeah?" questioned Anna. "I just wanna know... do you know anyone called Willow?" asked Twylar quietly. "Uhm.. yeah.. she kinda stole my two best friends away from me..." she muttered. "What were their names?" asked Twylar. "Mia and Melody, they're siblings", she answered. "Well... thanks... Good luck on your job as Queen!" said Twylar before she rushed off to Moon. "Where's Ava?" she asked. "Oh yeah, she went to go to the bathroom", replied Moon lazily as she slouched on the mint green couch. Twylar sat down by the fireplace, feeling its warmth. "Should I go reply back to the countries wanting to join us?" asked Twylar suddenly as she got up. She walked to the library and read all the letters sent her way. "The UK wants to join... accepted, America... accepted, Bangladesh..." muttered Twylar as she ran her fingers through the list and accepted everybody in. "Wow.. there's still a lot of countries left in the world.." wondered Twylar. You see, back in January 2008, the world started to experience some minor changes. Such as, China moved from the place it was before to next to America. Soon, some of the countries forged together and formed The Circle Of Kingdoms. So, there weren't a lot of the old countries left. Although only in The Circle of Kingdoms is there magic. "Should've asked that spirit of wisdom I met at the forest," thought Twylar.

The countries who had joined the Axis are: Canada, Africa and Japan. Of course, our heroes don't know this yet. The Legends all sat together, huddled up next to the fireplace, and Twylar told them who had joined the Allies. "Ok, so.. I'll just say everyone involved in it, ok?" began Twylar, "so there's us, The Legends, Spirit Forest, Bunny Town, Ever Green, America, the UK, and uh Bangladesh," Said Twylar, as she read from a list. Estella sniffed sadly next to Moon, who hugged her for support. Later in the future, South and North Korea joined the Allies, India, Russia and Pakistan too. But of course, The Legends hadn't received their letters yet. Suddenly, Anna came in to join them. "Alrighty! Ava, I've sent some spies to go investigate King William, to see what he's planning," announced Anna, as she sat next to Twylar.

She stared at the soft, mint green, £56,000 couch. And they were all sitting on the floor. Anna smiled at Estella in a way meant to calm her down. But clearly, it didn't work. "I.. need a moment", she sniffled. She ran off to the bathroom. "I feel bad.. the bunny king was the only one who cared about her when she was a kid... This whole experience must be so tough for her," said Twylar sadly. Soon, after 2 minutes, Estella came back. Twylar had just finished accepting the rest of the letters that came her way, so she set them aside and looked nervously at Estella. "Estella.. you can talk to us, y'know?" said Moon as she wrapped her arms around her. "I'm fine... I'm already forgetting about it.. see?" said Estella reassuringly, keeping on a fake smile. Knowing she wasn't being truthful, The Legends gave each other worried looks. "Estella.. don't fake smile, we're your friends!" said Ava, as she looked worriedly at her.

Everyone agreed. "Can we not, like.. talk about this now?" mumbled Estella. Feeling a storm of emotions brewing, Twylar quickly changed the subject. "Oh yeah... uh, didn't Anna send some bunny agents to The Isle Of Irene? I'm sure they've come back by now..." she realised as she beckoned for everyone to follow her. They reached the bunny agents as they came back, dressed in black suits. "What happened?" asked Alex, "America has recently found sightings of secret satellites in space, and they seem to belong to Dragon Thorn. Russia has interpreted the codes being sent from those satellites, and their President has kindly written it down." Said one of the agents as he pulled out a thin sheet of paper. He read it aloud: "Wait for two weeks, then attack, China is still gathering secret information. Do not make it clear that you will attack in two weeks." The bunny agent then bent down, ripped up the paper and set it on fire. "We can't have any evidence we have that-" explained the other bunny agent.

The Legends just nodded. "Hey, uh... Twy, I think you should spend the rest of the day with Camilla. You two haven't been together for like weeks," suggested Lily. Twylar nodded and ran off to find her. In the end, she found Camilla scoffing down all of the chocolates. "Camilla!" said Twylar cheerfully as she ran to hug her only living relative. She regarded her father as, well, not her father. If that made any sense. "Oh! 'wylar," said Camilla, with a mouth full of chocolate. She swallowed all of them, and they tumbled down her throat. "dear, dear, dear... I've eaten all of them!" she mumbled, as she inspected the now empty chocolate box. "Well, let's go grab something to eat, shall we?" suggested Camilla, as she led Twylar away to a place called 'Carrot Rush.'

Chapter Six

As they entered Carrot Rush, they saw that everything their eyes touched was either the colour orange or carrot-themed. Bunnies and carrots... what a beautiful love story. Twylar sat down at a table next to a family of bunnies. The father heftily lifted up the wailing baby and hushed it to sleep. Twylar thought of an old memory. She was 5 years old, and Twylar remembered as clear as day what had happened. King William, Queen Amber, Stacey, Christie and Twylar all travelled to the zoo one day. King William had left all his duties to the reliable adviser so that he could spend more time with his favourite daughters. (obviously, Stacey and Christie had to bring Twylar along, too, because Queen Amber insisted) Twylar remembers her mother's long blonde hair and her glistening amber eyes. They had decided to visit the lions first, seeing as it was Christie's favourite animal.

Next, they took a look at the mischievous monkeys, Stacey's favourite animal. The zoo had given them special access inside the animal's enclosures, supervised by a member of staff. Queen Amber led Twylar away from the monkeys and to the wolf enclosure. That would obviously have been Queen Amber's favourite animal, so she took Twylar inside the cage to see them more closely. King William and his two daughters watched in terror as they saw Twylar giggling with laughter as she pointed her little finger at the wolves. Stacey screamed. She was scared of wolves. Christie was brave enough to go near the glass, and she watched her mother hug one of the wolves. Suddenly, she stepped aside and let Twylar go in front of her. One of the biggest wolves there had steadily approached her, and Twylar let it come. "That's the alpha of this pack", explained Queen Amber. The great white wolf nuzzled his head against Twylar's hand, and she touched its furry forehead gently. The white wolf retreated into the shadows, and Twylar caught it smile warmly to her as she left the cage. "ENOUGH OF THIS NONSENSE!" yelled King William. They went back to the tiger cage, and the manager of Clover Lily Zoo watched over Christie like a hawk as she chased the tiger cubs around. Stacey watched in awe and soon went to join her. Twylar stood by her mother and listened to her father's words. Her 5-year-old mind could not understand why he was shouting but listened to it all the same. "Amber, my dear! You must stop helping Twylar clean!

You have your queen duties to attend to!" he roared. Amber nodded and spoke in a gentle voice to make him understand.

"What type of mother would I be, if I don't even help my child to nurture and grow? Since you won't give her a proper education, I will keep abandoning my duties to help my child." The king groaned. "If education is what you want, education is what you'll get! After today, Twylar will attend Sammy's school! What a good girl she is... no wonder my two girls are friends with her!" he sighed and took Christie away from the tigers. "Twylar! Food's ready!" said Camilla, waking her up from her memory.

As they ate at Carrot Rush, the rest of The Legends had a wild idea. "LET'S SURPRISE TWY WHEN SHE GETS BACK!!!!" yelled Zilas, waiting for everyone to yell 'YEAH!' they had agreed to act for her, but Ava had the perfect idea. "Ok so who's the best here at acting like a ghost?" she asked, Moon put her hand up. "Excellent! Let's go to that maze thingy not far from here, Estella showed me where it was." Continued Ava as she led The Legends out of the castle. "Moon, put on this blanket and stay in the entrance of the maze!" commanded Ava, as she handed Moon a white blanket. "Ok," she agreed as she waddled over to the beginning of the maze. Back in Carrot Rush, Camilla and Twylar had finished their meal. "Who knew Carrot cookies could be so good?" questioned Camilla as she looked back. "Oh well, run along now, Twylar! I think you're having a meeting soon." Finished Camilla. "A meeting!? Already?" thought Twylar as she ran to the castle. She could not find her friends in the meeting room or anywhere else! So, deciding that she should see if they were in the castle meadows, she ran across the main hall and found them there. Of all places, the meadows. "This place is infested with wasps..." she thought darkly as she tried to avoid a particularly large wasp nest.

All The Legends had their backs to Twylar, "MOON GOT LOST IN A MAZE!!" sniffled Ava, suddenly turning to face Twylar. "What?? Let's go find her then!" said Twylar, clearly worried for her friend. Alex bit back his laughter and turned to face Twylar, too. "C'mon! Let's go find her together!" he suggested as he ran off. Once they were outside the castle, Alex navigated them out of all the city cars and noises and out onto an open field. In the middle of that field was a mossy, crumbling wall of stone. "It's too high! I can't fly above it..." murmured Twylar as she stared up at the ancient building. Half of it was unseen as it was covered by clouds! Suddenly, something that looked like a person underneath a heavy, fluffy white blanket appeared from the entrance of the maze, and it charged straight for Twylar. "AAAAAAAAHH!!!!" she screamed, but the ghost screamed too. Wondering what was wrong, Twylar looked behind her and saw at least 12 clones of her, lifeless. The ghost pulled off the white blanket to reveal a very sweaty Moon. "That... hah... blanket... was so... hah... heavy..." she huffed. But they were not listening. They were all staring at Twylar's clones. "Uhm... why aren't they moving?" wondered Twylar. She had recovered from her state of shock when she first saw the ghost, but now she wanted payback. She tried to get the clones to move, but in the end, she couldn't. Finally, she thought of one of them moving, and it did. "Cool!!" she wondered out loud. The 'ghost' held out its sweaty arm to grab a bottle of water from Lily.

Suddenly, the fog chose that this was the right time to appear, which was good for Twylar as she could blend in with the clones. The fog was quick to disperse, and all Twylar's clones attacked the moment it did. "OK, OK! I'M SORRY!!" yelled Moon, as she found all the clones were chasing her only. "pfffffffffffttttttt" choked Lily, as she held in her laughter. "BWAHAHAHAAH" laughed Ava, a tear rolling down her cheek. "Wait... you can cry even when you're happy!?" realised Zilas, as he saw the tear roll down Ava's cheek. Twylar thought of all the clones disappearing, and they did. She was greeted by a white, furry tail embedded with bright yellow gems.

Still conscious of her missing human ears, she felt on top of her head. It was still weird to find that wolf-like ears were on top of her head. "Right... I'm a werewolf..." she thought. She pictured some big hairy wolf standing on its hind legs, and then she thought of herself. "This isn't what I imagined werewolves to look like..." she thought, as she helped Moon up. The next day, Twylar decided she would spend more time with Camilla. After all, she was like a second mother to her! She climbed out of bed, got dressed and told Ava what she was going to do. Ava had her long blue hair down, which was a surprise to Twylar as she usually had it in a ponytail. "Alright, have fun Twy!" she said, as she put her hair into a ponytail. Twylar sped off to Camilla's room, knocked at least 20 times and barged in. "Why so energetic?" laughed Camilla, she too had just finished changing. Her straight black hair was left the only thing to tidy; her fringe was placed messily on top of her forehead. She was wearing a white cap, and she handed Twylar a baseball bat. "Let's play some baseball, K?" she suggested, smiling as she said so.

Now, I can't exactly describe what happened from that point onwards, well I can. Chaos. Destruction. All those things. Twylar broke her bat the first time, and when she was given a new one, she accidentally whacked the instructor in the eye with it. It had soon turned night, and Camilla thanked the instructor for putting up with their nonsense. Once Twylar had changed out her clothes, untied her hair and collapsed onto her bed, she drifted off into a peaceful sleep. She awoke in a familiar place. The white nothingness. "Mum?" she asked, her voice echoing. Suddenly, Queen Amber came through the mist, and in front of Twylar. "My dear..." she sobbed as she hugged her daughter. "What happened?" asked Twylar as she wrenched herself free from her mother's grasp.

Chapter Seven

Queen Amber rubbed her eyes and began to speak. "There is a lot I have just recently found out, dear", she began. "The king has the blossom of hope, one of the things needed to begin the life of the next tree. The one that imprisoned Camilla..." she paused to hiccough, then continued. "There are two other things... the Ocean's heart and one spirit soul." She said wearily. "But mum, we've got the Ocean's heat!" reasoned Twylar. "Yes, dear, but there is another powerful alternative. If the tree was made using that sceptre... not even cutting down the tree would free you..." she said darkly. "What sceptre?" questioned Twylar as she raised her eyebrows. "The demon lord's sceptre. He is not real, but the locals have just started calling the sceptre that because of its unreal abilities. Once in the wrong hands... there may be no chance of stopping dear William..."

Twylar widened her eyes. "The demon lord's sceptre... sounds like a name straight from a dragon quest..." she murmured. "My dear, there were only two people in this world who knew the location of the sceptre. One was me, and the other was a retired farm worker who is currently living with his daughter and her children. His memory may not be good, and it will be a hassle locating him. Which is why I'm going to tell you where it is." She began, "Travel to a village in Volcano Hills called Mai'ho; it should be somewhere there." She finished.

Twylar thought about her mother's words carefully and nodded. "You may go now, dear..." murmured Queen Amber. Then, Twylar awoke. She tried to fall back asleep again, seeing as it was one in the morning. Failing to do so, she climbed out of bed and put on her coat. As she pulled on her boots, she decided that a walk in the woods would be nice. Yes, at one in the morning. The good thing would be that no one would be awake. As she stealthily crept to the castle gate, she thought about her mother's words. As she neared the path of the forest, it reminded her heavily of the Spirit Forest. As she walked further into the forest, the path began to fade. "Oh well. If I get lost, I can just fly above everything," thought Twylar as she ventured deeper into the tangled forest.

Twylar walked with her hands in her pockets, staring at the trees all around her. Her long hair flowed down. As she walked, her eyes caught sight of a moving shadow. Not wanting to worry herself, she pretended as though she had not seen anything. After her walk, she took her time to make her way back to the castle. She only slept the entire day and night. When she finally woke up, Ava had announced something. "You had a fever, but I think you were healing yourself by sleeping for an entire day!" she said as she sat next to Twylar. "Isn't that normal?" she asked as she gulped down the hot soup brought to her. "Yes, but you managed it in one day!" said Ava, proudly. "Well, since you're good to go... Camilla's agreed to host our first-ever Legends tournament! Well, it's not really... it's just some test of bravery," admitted Ava. "Sure, I'll join..." said Twylar wearily, imagining all the things that would happen. She and her friends had gathered at the entrance of the woods, the place she'd visited just a night before. "THE TEST OF BRAVERYYY!!" shouted Camilla as she stood in front of them.

She smiled at Twylar before continuing. "Alrighty... team A is Twylar, Alex and Ava!" the three were already standing in a group nearby, "Team B is Zilas, Lily, Moon and Estella." She finished. "Team B will go in first; remember, your goal is to scare Team A!" she shouted as Team B ran off into the forest. "Team A, on my... uhm... when I clap, you guys go in!" Camilla fumbled around for her whistle but realised she wasn't carrying one now. When she clapped, Team A dashed into the forest. As soon as they entered, a barrier formed around the forest, trapping them inside. "Well done, Z.." thought Twylar darkly, knowing she couldn't leave now. "Well, come on! Ignore that wolf howls- "stuttered Ava. "Yeah, it's just Moon" realised Alex. As they walked on further, Twylar couldn't help but feel watched.

The shadow followed, and soon Twylar had enough. She crept to the bushes, indicating for Alex and Ava to stay quiet. She kicked the bush violently, and something jumped out. "Oh! Just a squirrel..." laughed a very relieved Twylar. "LOOK OUT!!" shouted Ava as she pushed Twylar out of the way. "Long time no see, sis," said a very arrogant voice. "Christie..." said Twylar, anger and hatred penetrating every word she spoke. "Oi, where's your goons at?" she spat, looking around. "Dealing with your freaky friends" smirked Christie. Twylar could see that not far from her and Christie, Sammy's raw strength clashed against Ava's sword, and Stacey mercilessly attacked Alex.

93

Christie smirked once again. "Listen, my dearest younger sister, let's fight. I've been itching... I was the one who begged Dad... haha, yes..." she laughed to herself before continuing. "I want to be the one to end you. The one that ends the entire werewolf race!" she laughed before clenching her fists. "what's the matter, baby? No want fight big sissy?" she said in a childish voice. Twylar grumbled angrily and let her emotions control her. She led with a kick, dodging all of Christie's attacks. "You see, I was fed one of the petals of the blossom of hope. Sammy and Stacey, too. What they don't know is that I ate two extras." Christie smiled a devilish grin. Suddenly, her fist contacted Twylar's face. She felt as though it was over... the end was near. Twylar's body thumped on the floor, flowers were covering every aspect of her body. It was over. She did not have enough energy to heal. "And that's my special flower punch! My poisonous little blossoms should be infecting your stomach as we speak." Laughed Christie.

It was true; Twylar could feel something in her stomach; it hurt. "Now they should be entering your brain!" said Christie merrily, skipping in delight. "3... 2.." before she hit one, Twylar had blacked out. She was dead. "Oh... you're that weak?" Christie didn't even seem to care. "That's enough, girls. Retreat!" she ordered. "THE BARRIER ALEX! WE CAN STILL CATCH THEM!!" realised Ava, "T-twy.." said Alex, his eyes staring at the gruesome but pretty sight. "Those flowers are beautiful, Twy, but get up now" yawned Ava, clearly not realising what happened. The barrier closed; Team B had won. "Wait... is she... is..." stuttered Ava, sitting next to Twylar's lifeless body.

Alex quietly nodded and watched as Ava burst into tears. Mournfully and still holding back tears, Ava carried Twylar out of the forest. Once the sun was on their skin, they explained the whole situation with tears invading their eyelids. "Those brats..." said Lily angrily, choking back tears. "Go find them!" Moon commanded, and a small robin nodded its tiny head. Camilla was just standing there, staring at Twylar's body. It was covered in flowers. She did not appear to be crying, however, instead, she was smiling.

Chapter Eight

Twylar was not dead. Well, not yet. "My child?" said Amber as she ran to her daughter. "Wha-" began Twylar. How was this possible? She was dead, wasn't she? "Yes, dear, you were lying on the ground a couple seconds ago." Amber finished her sentence for her. "Wait... will you be able to revive me, mum?" asked Twylar. "No, dear, I cannot" she replied. "But there is someone who can... someone who lives inside you", she continued, "you may meet them any second now. They might be good or bad, for I have never personally met them." She admitted. She planted a kiss on Twylar's forehead and disappeared.

Suddenly, Twylar saw what looked like the same eyes Twylar saw before she was transformed, deep purple eyes stared into hers. She didn't even have time to react. As she was replaying her mother's words in her head, still struggling to understand the information. Something lived inside her? Wasn't her mother the only soul living inside her? When her mother transferred her powers to her, a fragment of her soul was transferred into Twylar's body but... was there something else hiding inside her? Twylar shuddered at the thought. 'They may be good or bad' Twylar kept thinking back to that phrase, deciding whether she thought that thing was good or bad. That was when she realised the purple-eyed thing was still there.

It stared into her eyes, and suddenly Twylar felt herself spinning... and spinning... her head was getting lighter, and she could hear her heart beating fast. She was falling. She was going to hit the ground. But she was dead, wasn't she? She opened her eyes and found herself somewhere unfamiliar. It wasn't the forest or her bedroom. It looked like a hospital, but the roof was very close to Twylar's head. And the thing is, she was lying down. A bunny wearing a nurse uniform shuffled over towards the door, not realising she was awake. Just then, someone came in. "Camilla!" muttered Twylar, finding herself unable to move her mouth. Camilla ushered the bunny out and sat down in a chair next to Twylar's bed. Her thoughts still centred on what her mother had said, and she tried yet again to speak. It didn't work. Somehow, Camilla seemed to realise she was awake, but she didn't look surprised. "Ah! You're a little fighter, aren't you? I thought it would take at least 5 days!" smiled Camilla, helping Twylar up.

 "Do you really think I should be standing up right now?" muttered Twylar, still unable to move her mouth freely. "Your mother's very good in healing; she's a light amethyst." Explained Camilla, "My mum? But... she said she couldn't do it?" wondered Twylar, her mouth still paralysed. "Ny nun? Speak properly, for goodness' sake!" laughed Camilla. "Not my fault my mouth can't move..." muttered Twylar, which Camilla had translated as: "No' ny faul' ny nout' can' moof.."

After Twylar had regained her strength and could talk properly again, Camilla covered Twylar in a blanket and pretended that she was someone else. "Oi! Whas' under dat?" spat a harassed-looking receptionist, "Sorry! Uhm... Lucy's allergic to sunlight!" shouted Camilla as she directed Twylar out of the hospital. Once safely out of sight of anyone they might happen to meet, Twylar took the blanket off. "What's that for?" Twylar pointed at the blanket she had thrown on the floor. "I expect old Willy to know about your death by now... so, let's not make a fuss about you being alive, eh?" shrugged Camilla, picking up the blanket. "Willy?" asked Twylar, a look of confusion masked her face. "That's what I used to call my brother... had the same name," reasoned Camilla as she beckoned for Twylar to follow her.

Twylar reasoned with herself, "I should tell Camilla.." she thought.

"No... mum might not have wanted me to tell her..." she argued back.

"Ughh, let's just tell her!" she snapped, "You know what, I'll tell her tomorrow." Twylar had made up her mind and ran to catch up with Camilla.

Once they made it to the castle without detection, Twylar was asked to wait in her room and not make any sounds. She waited. And waited. Still no sign of anyone ever coming in, she sighed. Staring absent-mindedly out her window, she didn't realise Camilla had sneakily swept into the room. "Twylar!" she whispered. She directed her out of the room before continuing. "C'mon! I told them I got them presents- "admitted Camilla, hurrying Twylar outside. "What was the point of coming into the castle if we're going out?" wondered Twylar. She made it outside to the castle gardens.

The castle garden was quite big, it was not like the other gardens of the castle. On the left side of the garden, there was an oak tree. Surrounding that oak tree were various flowers blooming from the tree's roots. The path connected the garden to the library. The garden was in the middle of the castle, and trees were shading them from the sun's rays. On the right side of the garden, there was a small fountain with a diamond glinting at the top of it; not far from that fountain were two trees. Those trees had a small swing attached from one of the branches. A small clearing was just behind the fountain, and that was where The Legends were waiting.

Just their luck, the wind had become more violent. "Seems like there's a storm coming!" realised Camilla as she navigated Twylar (who was under a blanket) to the small clearing. "Everyone!" announced Camilla, her hands on her hips. Camilla whipped the blanket off Twylar dramatically. "I'M BACK!!" beamed Twylar, but stopped as she stared at her friends' faces. Ava's silky light blue hair tossed violently in the wind as she stared her 'dead' friend down. Zara looked Twylar up and down, still in disbelief. "TWY!?" yelled Alex, his jaw practically touched the ground. "Uhm... so... how long have I been dead?" said Twylar, hastily changing the subject. "About 3 years," joked Moon. "WHAAAAAT!?" screamed Twylar, now she was the one in disbelief.

Camilla sighed, "She's joking. It's been 2 days", she revealed. "Wait, we have 3 more days until we fight the king", realised Zilas. Alex looked at Twylar, "WE MISSED YOU TWY!!" he sobbed. Twylar sighed. She stared at everyone's shocked faces. Moon seemed the only one who was calm! "Twy, do you wanna come with me to visit Luna?" asked Moon once they were walking back. Estella had put her invisibility on a bracelet, and she had given it to Twylar. Meaning that she was now invisible. "Sure!" whispered Twylar. Twylar followed Moon to Bunny Bakery and climbed the stairs leading to the Evers' apartment. Once they were inside (Moon had the keys), Twylar took off her bracelet and found she was herself again. I think I should explain more about Estella's invisibility, even though it's very powerful, she cannot make other human beings invisible. Same with animals.

She can only make non-living things invisible, which works as an amulet as it makes the wearer invisible. Once Twylar had taken off her bracelet, Luna came running to Moon. She turned her head and realised Twylar was there. Luna stared at her, which Twylar thought was a bit weird. "Oh right, I'm supposed to be dead", realised Twylar as Luna squeezed her half to death. "Twylar, dear!" exclaimed Zoey Evers, her voice shaking. "Before you ask mum, magic!" said Moon before Mrs Evers could even ask how Twylar was alive. This was not as funny as Moon had thought it to be. "Magic? BLACK MAGIC?" fumed Mrs Evers, "No mum, ugh… you never get my jokes…" murmured Moon. "Oh, right… well, Mr Evers shall be wanting to see you." Mentioned Mrs Evers as she led Twylar to the kitchen. There, Mr Evers was attempting to feed all three of Moon's younger brothers at once.

One toddler spat out its food at its father's face, the other vomited on the floor, and the last sat obediently eating its risotto. Mr Evers was quite handsome. He had light brown hair like all his children, which he tied in a short ponytail because it was too long. His olive-green eyes stared down with disgust at the floor. His freckles were visible but faint, and his skin was tanned. Mrs Evers had light brown hair too, but she had dyed half of it white saying that it was 'style' (Moon cringed at this). Mr Evers had just realised that Twylar was there, as he jumped up from his chair in surprise. "What the "he began, wearing the same shocked face as everyone Twylar had seen. "Don't ask, dad." Interrupted Moon. Later that day, Twylar was helping Moon make dinner. Mr and Mrs Evers were busy watching over Moon's younger siblings, and the chaos of Twylar's arrival had deceased. "Chop those carrots up, Twy," commanded Moon as she expertly tipped the remainder of her chopped garlic into a pan. Twylar did as she was told and handed the small cut-up carrots to Moon. "What about the onions?" she asked, holding her hand out for a spatula.

Twylar swept across the room to retrieve a red, glossy spatula. She delivered it to Moon, who started doing expert chef things with it. Twylar wouldn't know. She's not the chef here! Twylar handed Moon a plate of badly chopped onions; she sighed and chopped it herself before tipping it into the pan. "Go set the table, please, Twy," asked Moon as she lazily stirred the contents of the pan.

    "Hey, it's kinda weird to be staying in one place, y'know" admitted Twylar. Moon raised an eyebrow.

"What d'you mean?" she asked, stopped stirring the pan now.

"We've been in Bunny Town for so long!" laughed Twylar as she

 headed to the dining room.

Moon shrugged and continued stirring the pan until the steak was brown.

Chapter Nine

Once dinner was ready, Twylar handed the knives and forks out, and they began to eat. "Thank you very much. We had planned to have pasta tonight, but this steak is exceptional!" said Mrs Evers with a smile. Moon swelled with pride. Mr Evers was having trouble feeding the triplets again; they all spat their baby food into his face! "Twy, no offence, but how did you—"Moon began. Twylar let out an audible sigh. She was hearing the same things over and over again.

Moon stopped abruptly, knowing what the answer would be. "Alright, I'll go put the triplets to bed then", announced Mr Evers, standing up with three toddlers in his arms. Mrs Evers kissed him on the cheek, and Moon paid more attention to her fork than to her parents while they were doing this. A few hours later, the Evers family had kindly let Twylar stay with them. Since she was so used to her familiar silk floral bed back in the Bunny Castle; the battered beige sofa felt like a stranger. From where she was, she could hear someone snoring and small feet scurrying towards the kitchen. She stood up and decided to investigate.

As she walked to the kitchen, she could see a shadow of someone opening the fridge. Twylar kept quiet in case it was an intruder. "Oh! It's just you!" sighed Twylar, realising it was just Luna. "Sorry, did I make too much noise?" she asked, a packet of crisps dropped from her full arms. "Let me help with that," mumbled Twylar as she bent down to pick up the crisp packet. "Barbecue chicken? Never heard of that!" remarked Twylar as she read from the packet. "It's a really good flavour, I recommend it!" smiled Luna as she took the packet off Twylar. "Well, see you in the morning!" and with that, Luna hurried to her room. Twylar yawned and headed back to her couch. A few hours had passed, yet Twylar couldn't fall asleep. Just one more day. Well, the plan is that she would have to be hidden; the King wasn't supposed to know she was still alive!

Her eyelids grew heavy, and the night seemed endless, each minute crawling by as Twylar lay on the beige couch. The dim glow of the streetlights seeped through the curtains, casting eerie patterns on the walls. She turned onto her side, trying to find a comfortable position, but the realisation that she would soon meet... *him* kept her mind occupied. Her mind had not forgotten about their last fight— he had almost won...

She closed her eyes and took deep breaths, attempting to calm her racing heart. Back home, Queen Amber would have stayed in her old, shabby tower until Twylar fell asleep, but now that was impossible.

As Twylar's mind drifted into a restless slumber, she found herself transported back to a familiar place—the school playground. She was younger now—vulnerable and alone. Christie, Sammy, and Stacey stood before her, their faces twisted into cruel smiles as they laughed and pointed at her. Their laughter echoed around the playground, soon joined by the other children's mocking voices. Twylar felt her cheeks burn with humiliation, her heartache deepened by the absence of her friends, who were currently in detention. She stood there, enduring the torment, drowning in a sea of negative emotions, feeling utterly isolated.

When the first light of dawn crept through the windows, Twylar finally managed to get a few moments of sleep. The aroma of freshly brewed coffee and sizzling sausages soon filled the house, rousing her from her uneasy slumber. She stretched and reluctantly got up from the beige sofa, making her way to the dining room where the Evers family was gathered for breakfast.

"Good morning, Twylar!" greeted Mrs. Evers with a warm smile. "Did you sleep well?"

Twylar returned the smile and nodded, even though she felt far from rested. "Morning, everyone. The breakfast smells amazing!"

Mr. Evers handed her a plate filled with eggs, sausages, and toast. "Help yourself, Twylar. You'll need your strength."

As they ate, the room buzzed with lively conversation and laughter. The triplets, now much more cooperative, babbled happily in their highchairs. Twylar felt a pang of sadness, knowing she would soon leave this loving household behind.

After breakfast, Twylar stood at the door, ready to say her goodbyes. She hugged each member of the Evers family, saving Luna for last. "Thank you for everything," she said, her voice tinged with emotion.

Luna hugged her tightly. "Take care of yourself, Twy. And remember, you're always welcome here."

Twylar's heart ached at the thought of the welcome she'd receive from her father if she were to suddenly appear at his doorstep. With a final wave, Twylar left the Evers' house and made her way to the Bunny Castle. The day was bright and crisp, the perfect backdrop for her last day of freedom. She was determined to make the most of it, pushing aside the anxiety about the next day.

As she approached the castle, she was greeted by her friends—Alex, Estella, Moon, Zilas, Lily, and Ava—who had already started preparing for the New Year's Eve celebration. The castle was buzzing with excitement, and decorations adorned every corner.

"Welcome, Twy!" shouted Alex, pulling her into a bear hug. "We've got a big party planned for tonight!"

The day flew by in a whirlwind of activities. They decorated the grand hall, set up tables laden with delicious food, and arranged a dance floor for the evening's festivities. As the sun dipped below the horizon, the castle transformed into a magical wonderland, ready to ring in the new year.

That night, everyone from the castle gathered to celebrate. The air was filled with music, laughter, and the clinking of glasses. Twylar danced with her friends, her worries melting away with each step. They watched in awe as fireworks lit up the sky, their vibrant colours reflecting in their eyes.

For a few precious hours, Twylar forgot about the challenges that awaited her. Surrounded by friends and joy, she embraced the moment, letting the magic of the night carry her away. Together, they welcomed the new year with hope and excitement, ready to face whatever the future might hold.

"To 2026!" laughed Twylar, holding up her cup. A smile lingered upon her lips.

"To 2026!" everyone yelled. The entire staff had been invited—even the new Queen! They danced their worries away, and The Legends had stayed past midnight! The bad thing was, as they were the only ones left, it was their responsibility to clean. The party had somewhat stained the ballroom's reputation, a space more commonly used for ballerinas to twirl and glide across the room.

Alex, with a determined look, began cleaning the ballroom quickly using his levitation powers. The debris and confetti from the celebration floated into neat piles, guided by his precise control. His friends watched in admiration before they hurried back to their rooms, eager for some rest.

However, the night was far from over. They decided to have one last gathering in Lily's room, where the atmosphere was cosy and warm. The room, adorned with soft lights and plush cushions, became their sanctuary. They chatted animatedly about the day's events and their plans for the next.

"Can you believe how magical that night was?" Lily said, her eyes shining with excitement.

"It was unforgettable," Moon replied, nodding. "But now we have to get ready for tomorrow."

The conversation soon turned serious as they discussed the challenges that lay ahead. King William, Twylar's father, mostly known as a cruel, heartless man, had killed his own wife because she was a werewolf. Twylar, therefore, was the princess of The Isle of Irene, a title she didn't want.

"I've been so worried about tomorrow," Twylar admitted, her voice barely above a whisper. "But now, I feel a bit more confident."

Her friends offered words of encouragement, reassuring her that she was more than capable of handling her duties. As the night grew late, Twylar found herself drifting into an easy sleep, the worries of the previous night seeming almost silly in hindsight. She knew she would do well. After all, it wasn't as daunting as it seemed. All she had to do was wear a wig to cover her distinctive hair, a mask to hide her face, and a black hoodie to blend into the shadows. Her main task was to protect the spirits from the King's soldiers, who on his command, fought for the spirit souls.

As she closed her eyes, she felt a wave of determination wash over her.

The next day, Twylar woke up early, the dawn light filtering through her window, casting a golden hue across her room. She quickly ate breakfast, a simple yet hearty meal that provided her with the energy she needed for the day ahead. Her mind was already racing with the tasks that lay before her. She hurriedly woke her friends, gently shaking them from their slumber. They sleepily nodded their heads and began to prepare for the day, their movements slow but determined.

Together, they made their way to the spirit forest, a place shrouded in mystery and bathed in the ethereal glow of the early morning light. The forest was alive with the sounds of nature, the rustling leaves, the chirping of birds, and the distant murmur of a stream. It was a serene and magical place, and the spirit chief Paris smiled warmly at them.

Twylar, now disguised as Coral, wore a striking red wig that stood out vividly against the green foliage. Her usual appearance was completely altered. She wore heavy amounts of makeup to cover her black mark. She kept to the shadows, her movements stealthy and deliberate, her heart pounding with anticipation. She knew the King was near, and she had to be cautious.

As she navigated through the dense forest, her senses on high alert, the King suddenly appeared before her. His presence was imposing, and he studied her with a sneer of suspicion. "Who are you?" he demanded, his voice harsh and filled with contempt.

With a defiant snort, Twylar met his gaze unwaveringly. "I'm Coral, a replacement for Twylar. And I'll *end* you! Even if it's the last thing I do," she declared, her voice steady and resolute.

Before the King could react, she vanished into the shadows, her form blending seamlessly with the darkened forest. The King was left bewildered and incensed, his mind racing with confusion and anger. Determined not to be outdone, he ordered his soldiers to gather the spirit souls, their orders clear and unwavering. At the same time, he and a contingent of his fiercest warriors prepared to confront The Legends, their resolve steeled for the battle ahead.

The forest quickly transformed into a battleground, the air filled with the sounds of clashing swords, battle cries, and the haunting wails of spirits. Twylar, hidden and watchful, observed the chaos that unfolded before her. She knew she had to act to protect the spirits and her friends, to fulfil her mission, no matter the cost. Her heart swelled with determination and courage as she vowed to do whatever it took to ensure their safety.

Eyeing a particular soldier who was nearing too close to the spirit forest, Twylar slashed out her sword (she couldn't use her powers, or it would be obvious) and watched as the soldier's helmet slashed in two. Ava's sword seemed to be working well for her. Well, that was because Ava had given Twylar full-on permission! She wasn't worried, though, as she knew Ava could fight a whole army with bare hands and still *win*.

Suddenly, a small spirit child darted out from the underbrush, eyes wide with fear as a soldier drew near, his sword raised menacingly. Without a moment's hesitation, Twylar leapt forward, her own sword flashing in the dappled light. The soldier turned just in time to see the glint of steel before Twylar struck, her blade slicing through his armour with precise force.

The soldier staggered back, stunned, as his armour clattered to the ground in pieces, leaving him revealed, wearing something Twylar didn't expect—hello kitty pyjamas. The sight was so absurd that for a moment, both Twylar and the spirit child stared in disbelief. The spirit child giggled, pointing at the soldier's pyjama-clad legs, while Twylar had to bite her lip to stifle her laughter. The soldier, his face flushing with embarrassment, made a hasty retreat, his earlier menace completely shattered.

As he ran, his oversized pyjama bottoms began slipping down, revealing cartoonish pink fluffy slippers that squeaked with every hurried step. Twylar couldn't help but chuckle as the spirit child clapped their hands in delight, shouting, "Run, Mr Kitty!" The now thoroughly humiliated soldier tripped over a root, somersaulted, and landed in a pile of leaves, his slippers flying off and landing in a nearby stream.

Twylar quickly gathered the small spirit into her arms, her heart pounding with both adrenaline and relief. She whispered comforting but unnecessary words to the child, seeing as he was giggling ferociously. After a final glance at the humiliated soldier, she allowed the spirit child to return to his mother and resumed her position in the trees. Afraid that her flaming red wig would attract the attention of nearby soldiers, Twylar shuffled a little further into the leaves of a tree she was hiding in.

As Twylar got herself back together, she noticed a sudden change in the atmosphere. The air got tense, and the battle sounds paused for a moment. Out of the forest shadows came three figures—Paris, Winter, and Eris, each bringing their unique flair to the scene.

Eris, with her goat horns, elf ears, and green lizard tail, was the spirit of discord. Her eyes sparkled with mischief as she locked onto the king. With a flick of her hand, the ground under the king started to rumble. He tried to keep his balance, but the earth eventually gave way, swallowing him whole. The soldiers rushed to help him, but Eris was ready. With a mischievous grin, she used her magic to pull their pants down and hang them by their underwear from the tree branches. The soldiers flailed helplessly, trying their best to hide themselves from humiliation.

Winter, with her icy demeanour, sent a frosty wind that froze another group of soldiers solid. The chill was intense, and they seemed trapped for a bit. But with a lot of effort, they managed to break free, moving sluggishly and shivering from the cold.

Paris, the chief and probably the strongest of all spirits, joined The Legends in their fight against the king and his forces. His sword flashed in the dim light as he blocked blows and struck with anger. The combined efforts of Eris, Winter, and Paris created a fierce force, pushing back the king's army with relentless determination.

The battlefield turned into a crazy mix of chaos and shouts, with the spirits and their allies working together to protect their forest and friends. Twylar felt a rush of pride and hope as she watched the strength and bravery of her friends and wished she was down there with them.

She couldn't take it anymore. She wished she side along fighting with her friends, and she wished she could show that... *man* that she hated him with all her guts. Taking a deep breath, she let her emotions control her. She jumped down from the tree.

"Twy- I mean, Coral!" stammered Ava as she looked behind to see Twylar running towards the dangerous landmine they were fighting in.

"MIND THOSE ICE SHARDS TW- CORAL!" yelled Winter, looking over her shoulder. "I'll give this stupid, brainless, sulky little maniac a taste of his medicine..." Twylar muttered darkly, eyeing King William with a look of venom. She whipped off her wig, ripped off her mask and smiled as she saw King William stare at her as though she were a ghost. "Boo!" she yelled. She laughed as half of the remaining of the King's men fled, clearly convinced she *was* a ghost.

The King regained his thoughts and snorted his usual snort. "Ah... so Christina failed me then... no worries, she'll get stronger over time." He sneered, eyeing the forgotten red wig lying two feet away from him. "Coral, Coral... should've known it was *you* of all people. What type of loser goes around saying, 'I'll end you?' well, you, of course!" he snorted.

"Says the man who killed his own wife!" said Twylar through gritted teeth.

"Hah? Oh right... that dog... well, she wasn't human anyway!" reasoned the king.

Twylar charged towards the king, her eyes burning with fury. The battlefield around her echoed with the clashing of swords and shouts of her friends. In the heat of the battle, Alex and Lily noticed Twylar's desperate struggle and decided to join her.

"Let's help her out!" Alex shouted to Lily. Without hesitation, they slipped into Twylar's fight. Lily's form shimmered and grew, transforming into a giant Siren. She towered over the battlefield like a tank. She knew if she sang, she would kill her friends too, so instead of singing, she picked up the king with her immense strength and threw him across the field. The king landed with a thunderous crash, sending a cloud of dust into the air.

Angered, the king summoned a monstrous giant unlike the mini versions of it Twylar had seen before; it climbed from a dark portal in the ground and stood in front of Lily. The creature was a horrifying amalgamation of the skull of a deer, the body of an ape, and the legs of a tiger. It let out an ear-splitting roar and charged towards Lily, who stood her ground.

Meanwhile, Alex gaped at the giants fighting not far from them. "TWY!" he yelled, and they both coordinated their attacks with precision. They moved like a well-oiled machine, striking the king from different angles. Twylar's agility let her dodge and weave, landing swift blows, while Alex's strength made every punch feel like a hammer. The king, overwhelmed by their relentless assault, struggled to keep up, angered that someone he hated was beating him.

Just as they were about to deliver a final blow, a panicked soldier rushed to the king's side, shouting, "Your Majesty, we've collected two spirit souls!" The king's eyes widened in surprise and realisation. He quickly retreated, calling off his forces with a hasty wave. "Bye-bye!" he sneered, knowing they had won the battle, but he had won the war.

Twylar and Alex attempted to chase after King William, their hearts pounding with the thrill of battle. The adrenaline still coursing through their veins, they glanced around the battlefield, taking in the sight of their friends regrouping and celebrating small victories. They had shown their strength and unity, but they knew this was only a temporary reprieve. The king would undoubtedly return, and when he did, they would be ready to face him once more, or so Twylar hoped. The battle was over.

Alex looked over his shoulder and saw that Paris was crying. "They didn't take just two spirit souls..." explained Moon as she bent down to comfort Paris. "They... they took five?" guessed Twylar, Moon nodded shakily. "The spirits of Goodwill, charity, fire, water and sun... are gone", revealed Winter. Twylar held back tears. If she had just stayed in her post... maybe then the king wouldn't have those 5 spirit souls... maybe then the chance of the tree growing again would be slim. The bad thing was the king only needed one spirit soul. More spirit souls probably meant more power. "It's okay though, right? I mean, we won't lose the sun because its spirit's gone?" asked Alex nervously. "No, another spirit must take on that role until we find another human to fulfil it..." stammered Paris. She had stopped crying now.

Zilas looked bewildered. "You mean a bad human wandered here?" asked Estella. Paris nodded. "A good human can take the role if they are willing to." She revealed. "Well, you have done your best. If Twylar had not jumped in the fight, the king may have taken my soul too." Twylar felt a surge of pride rushes through her. Winter sighed and stifled a smile. "Oh my gosh! That's the first time I've seen you smile!" said Moon bluntly. Everyone chuckled.

Chapter Ten

Winter pulled a small, shiny bag from her cloak. "Twylar," she said, "take these jade seeds. They'll take you back to Bunny Castle." Twylar, still feeling the adrenaline from the battle, took the bag and nodded.

She opened the bag and took out three jade seeds, each one glowing softly. She placed them in her hand and felt a rush of magic. "Everyone, grab onto me," she said, her voice calm despite everything that had happened.

Her friends gathered around, each palcing a hand on her shoulder or arm. As soon as they were all connected, the seeds started to hum, and they were surrounded by a whirlwind of energy. It felt like they were spinning through the air, everything around them turning into a blur of colours and light.

Before they knew it, they felt a sudden jolt, and the ground beneath their feet became solid again. Opening their eyes, they found themselves back in the familiar surroundings of Bunny Castle. The warm glow of the enchanted lanterns and the ornate halls welcomed them back to their temporary home.

Remembering what her mother had said, they would have to travel to Mai'ho soon. She wasn't excited to meet Willow along the way, seeing as Mai'ho was a village in Volcano Hills.

"Guys?" asked Twylar. Ava turned her head round questioningly.

Twylar took a deep breath and explained about Mai'ho and the demon lord's sceptre.

Before they left for Volcano Hills, The Legends made their way to Queen Anna's chamber to say their last goodbyes. Queen Anna stood by the window, gazing out at the horizon. She turned to them with a warm smile.

Camilla, with tears in her eyes, stepped forward and embraced the queen tightly. "Bye..." she whispered. Queen Anna held her close.

The Legends packed their belongings quickly, each item a reminder of their journey so far. With everything in order, they gathered around Twylar, who pulled out the jade seeds once more. But they had already used the last of the seeds to get to Bunny Castle. Estella handed them bracelets while they clutched their belongings. Ones which they couldn't see, meaning when they put them on, they would become invisible themselves. They had travelled secretly; who knows where King William's spies are?

They caught a train just as it was leaving, with Zilas dangling from the back. Ava hauled him board, and they took off their bracelets—Zilas had accidentally thrown his away, thinking it was a spider). They were in a bottle green compartment; the paint was rusty at its end and was peeling off. The door was left open, seeing as they didn't have the key to lock it. Twylar didn't mind the harsh, cold wind—her thoughts were more occupied with Willow. They had been best friends the moment they met, but Willow had tossed it all aside once she heard about the war. A few hours had passed, and dusk was approaching. Everyone tried sleeping inside the mountains of apple barrels travelling in the compartment with them, Camilla was the only one with enough sense to lean against the barrels instead of worrying about getting lost in them. Twylar, however, couldn't sleep at all. She stood by the entrance, letting the cold wind whip at her hair. Her eyes stared above at the winking stars and watched as clouds lazily drifted by. She couldn't help thinking about various situations where she would meet Willow, one of them was Willow laughing at her with her new friends. Twylar shivered. Maybe it was time to step away from the entrance and hide away from the cold in the corner of the room?

 But her body stayed exactly where it was. She wanted to move, but she didn't want to at the same time. She found herself arguing with herself about moving to the corner, until Alex woke up. His white T-shirt was now covered in mud and what seemed like apple juice. Nearby, a perfectly cut half of an apple rolled by. "Ava's sword!" realised Twylar, she took the sword and returned it to its owner, then she sat next to the entrance again.

Alex rubbed his eyes. He yawned, then went to sit next to Twylar. "Still worried about the sceptre? Trust me, Twy, it'll be a breeze!" chimed Alex. He grimaced as a fresh wave of cold air slapped him in the face.

"No, it's not that... it's just... Willow," Twylar murmured. But she was pretty sure Alex only heard the word 'Willow.'

"So, what about her?" he asked suspiciously. He remembered when Twylar and Willow broke up, and she did not look happy.

"She... I..." Twylar was struggling to get her words out. That was funny. Her head was crammed full of thoughts and situations of Willow, and how they would meet. "I'm just afraid of her reaction..." she admitted.

Alex nodded and smiled. "Well, we'll be in disguises anyway!" he mentioned. Twylar smiled. She was glad she talked with Alex. Feeling as if a heavy load was lifted off her shoulder, she said goodnight to Alex and sleepily dragged herself to the corner of the compartment. There were no more cold slaps of wind in her face, so she could finally sleep in peace.

Twylar woke up to the gentle shake of Estella's hand on her shoulder. "Stay quiet," Estella whispered. Twylar nodded sleepily, rubbing her eyes and stretching her stiff limbs.

The train had come to a halt, and the first rays of dawn were peeking over the horizon. Estella led everyone off the train with cautious steps, the cold ground crunching beneath their feet as they alighted.

They made their way through the early morning fog, each breath visible in the chilly air. Soon, they found themselves at the mouth of a cave, its dark entrance barely discernible in the dim light. A low growl emanated from within, sending shivers down Twylar's spine.

Moon stepped forward, her serene expression belying the tension in the air. She raised her hands gracefully, her eyes fixed on the shadowy figure of the bear that emerged from the depths of the cave. Without uttering a single word, her fierce eyes flamed. The bear, momentarily pacified, turned and lumbered away, disappearing into the wilderness.

The Legends exchanged silent glances of gratitude towards Moon before entering the now-vacant cave. Camilla, smiling warmly, began handing out disguises to The Legends. Twylar was Coral once more and saw that her red wig sort of resembled Camilla's long black hair. Twylar put on her brown contact lenses to conceal her abnormal eyes. She used Camilla's face mask to hide the black mark on her left eye. She placed the cold, thin paper over her skin. "No one can tell!" remarked Lily. Twylar changed out her old clothes into a black hoodie, then pulled on some jeans. She came out of the darkness of the cave, and everyone approved. Now, it was Lily's turn. Once she came out of the cave, her hair was no longer black. She was wearing a curly, blonde wig and had hazel contact lenses on. "I'm Sarah!" she beamed, smiling ear to ear. "Nice! So, we have Coral and Sarah- Who next?" asked Camilla. Next, Moon slipped into the shadows and came out as "I'm Zoya!" she chirped, she had a short black ponytail, and she sported a fringe. She twirled the bits of hair hanging from behind her ear and waited for Camilla's approval. 'Zoya' was wearing shorts and different coloured socks, one was hot pink and the other a minty green.

Ava came out as Aria; she had dyed one of Moon's spare wigs orange and untied the ponytail. Her blue contact lenses reflected in the sun. "AH! MY EYES!" she squealed, she didn't dare look up after that. Then, Estella appeared as Mia, who had short brown hair and green contact lenses. Alex grumpily walked out of the cave; his very spiky black hair was covering his right eye. he was wearing a spiked collar, and every inch of him was covered in black. "I can see why he's grumpy..." murmured Estella. "Jack." He grumbled before walking off to join Twylar and the rest.

Zilas happily skipped out of the cave. His usual red bandana was nowhere to be found, and his curly blonde wig threatened to get soaked in the upcoming rain. "Charlie!" he revealed. Soon, it was Camilla who was last to change. She sighed and came out as "Amber!" she burst. She looked *exactly* like her, too. The same wavy blonde hair, the same amber eyes... Twylar really felt as if this was her mother standing in front of her. "Well, let's start off by enrolling you at a school here! Since I'm the adult here, I will be the mother." Announced Camilla. "What, all of us?" blurted out Ava.

"Yes!" smiled Camilla. "Except you, Alex. You're a cousin!" she pointed at Alex. He groaned miserably.

Soon, they found themselves walking behind Camilla to 'Austin High School for talented persons' or Austin for short. Twylar felt her heart drop she saw Willow pass by. Laughing. Smiling. Without *her*. They met up with the principal, a formidable, bulky woman. "Hmm... I'll take them." She concluded. "So, he's a cousin, correct?" she gestured towards Alex. "Well, if he is, I'll need his parent's permission not aunt's." Camilla gave a silent plea for help. "They gave you permission..." Twylar whispered, just loud enough so Camilla could hear. "Ah! Uh... his parents are... insane!" Camilla began, "Tortured to insanity, miss" Camilla added. The principal nodded but with pity. "Welcome in, young man." She said after a while.

With their new identities in place, the group was ready to start their new school life. They hurried off to their respective classes, eager yet anxious about fitting in.

Lily and Twylar found themselves in the same math class, but to their dismay, there were no free spots left. Twylar ended up having to sit next to Willow. Coral and Willow quickly bonded over the lesson, with Willow helping her with the tricky problems. Lily, however, felt increasingly left out as the class progressed.

During the break, Twylar reunited with The Legends, sharing a quick conversation before heading to lunch. At lunch, she chose to sit with Willow, deepening their newfound friendship.

As the school day ended, they returned to the cave. Twylar used her yellow flames to light a fire, bringing warmth to their makeshift home. They settled in for the night, each lost in their own thoughts.

As Twylar drifted off to sleep, a small smile played on her lips. She felt a glimmer of happiness at rekindling her friendship with Willow. But a pang of sadness followed as she realised it wasn't truly her who had regained the bond, but Coral, her new identity.

When it was finally time to head home, Willow held Twylar's arm to stop her from going. "Go without me, guys!" she called, and The Legends wearily dragged their feet towards their makeshift home.

Willow smiled, and Twylar understood that she was supposed to follow her. Soon, the day had turned to night, and Willow handed Twylar a small, spray can bottle. They were facing the school walls, and to her surprise, Willow began painting on the wall. "C'mon Coral, it's fun!" called Willow. Twylar held the spray bottle in her shaky hands. Should she trust Willow? What if she didn't paint on the wall, and Willow didn't want to be friends because of that? Twylar had already experienced losing Willow once, and she couldn't do it again disguised as someone else entirely. Taking a deep breath, Twylar drew a very small smiley face at the bottom of the wall, hoping that no teacher would notice it. "You can do better than that!" laughed Willow as she drew a bigger smiley face in the middle of the wall.

Twylar, looking around to see if a teacher was coming, drew a very fat bird next to Willow's smiley face. Willow nodded her head in approval, and on top of the bird, she drew a very fat person, which she labelled 'principal fatty'. Twylar laughed throatily, unsure if she should follow in Willow's footsteps. She knew it was wrong, but... Willow might be disappointed in Twylar, and... she would lose a friend for the second time. She didn't have a choice. AS Twylar was in the middle of drawing, she heard the scuffling feet of at least two people. Willow, struggling to contain her laughter, steered Twylar away from the teachers, who had discovered their wall. To Twylar's horror, the principal was one of them.

She stared at Willow's drawing of her, studied the handwriting closely and quickly turned to the teacher accompanying her. "Tomorrow, round up all the kids who write likes this," she said hoarsely.

"Yes, Miss Stanton!" The other teacher called as she hurried back inside the school. With a heavy ache in her heart, Twylar smiled dimly at Willow and began the walk home. When no one was looking, Twylar felt a wave of cold wash over her body, meaning she had paused time. It was better to pause time to walk all the way home so she could save time. Any later than now would mean unnecessary questions would be asked. Before going home, however, Twylar decided to take off her mask. Mai'ho was a village surrounded by a lake, meaning it was sort of like an island. Twylar dived into the lake, and she didn't care if her clothes were wet. She threw her red wig next to her eye contacts back on the land and ripped off her face mask. It was like her skin was freed of a heavy burden; she grimaced as a bit of the mask wouldn't come off her skin. She let herself drop beneath the cool water before rising again. She was stupid. Now, she would have to arrive at their obnoxious little cave, where everything smelled damp and a bit like mud, *wet*.

She groaned miserably. If only she could turn back time... well, she already had that big disappointment back in that warehouse. What was the point of wearing her contacts or her wig if her black mark was revealed? Not like anyone would see it though, she had paused time.

Feeling she would just have to endure the suffering of being wet all the way until home, she got out the water drenched all the way to her socks. Once she finally made it home, she put her wig and contacts carefully in Camilla's bag before rummaging through Ava's bag for spare clothes. Her shoes were wet, too, meaning that she had left behind wet footprints on the stone floor.

She groaned. "I'm stupid... Why didn't I pack extra?" She thought. She pulled out an extra school uniform and a T-shirt. She put her shoes next to the fire and put two blazing rocks inside each of them; that way, they would dry both inside and out. Sighing, she unpaused time. Zilas stared at the wet footprints. "GHOST!!!" he screamed and jumped onto Alex, who toppled over, which caused Camilla's bag to topple over, which made Twylar's eye contact fling itself into the yellow flames. Twylar hurriedly tried to blow the fire out, which wasn't useful as her flames lasted over a century.

"Finally home?" asked Ava strictly.

"Yeah, you took forever!" agreed Zilas as he stood up to readjust Camilla's bag.

"Sorry, I... Uh, had to take off the face mask, see?" Twylar pointed at her face.

Camilla sighed, "Alright, we'll have to see if this place has any eye contacts that look like your old ones. Oh, face masks too!" announced Camilla.

"So, what did Willow hold you back for?" asked Lily, helping herself to some bread as she sat next to Moon.

Twylar gulped. She was hoping she wouldn't have to answer this question. She decided to tell a white lie, making it seem like Willow was the bad guy here. Well, it wasn't like they would go ahead and ask Willow herself, right? But they would certainly ask questions if Twylar hung around Willow after this. She gulped and opened her mouth. "She asked if I could come shopping with her", lied Twylar.

She faked a yawn. "Y'know what, I'm tired... I'll just go to bed then, night!" she waved and went near the entrance of the cave. That was where she had slept the night before, so why not make it her usual spot?

After buying a few face masks and eye contacts, Camilla went to sleep, too.

The next day, it was like Twylar wasn't even a part of The Legends anymore! It was just like old times; she and Willow would whisper secrets during class, share lunch under the old oak tree, and laugh about their mischief. Twylar felt her guilt build up inside her, but she couldn't ruin this. She didn't want to lose her friend, yet the weight of last night gnawed at her.

One evening, as they gathered around the fire, Zilas broke the silence. "Twy, everything alright?" Twylar hesitated, then nodded. "Just adjusting to the new life, that's all," she replied, her voice barely above a whisper.

But secrets have a way of surfacing.

The next day, the school principal announced the vandalism during assembly. A chill ran down Twylar's spine. Willow squeezed her hand, feigning innocence. Twylar played along, but the fear of being exposed haunted her.

The principal continued, "We have zero tolerance for such behaviour. If anyone has information, come forward, and the matter will be dealt with seriously."

Twylar avoided eye contact with everyone, especially The Legends. She knew time was running out, and the burden of her actions felt heavier as every minute passed.

That night, unable to sleep, Twylar realised she had to decide. Would she continue down this path just for a friend, or would she come clean and face the consequences? She stared at the flickering flames, lost in thought, as the weight of her choices pressed down on her. The next day, she put on her second fake mask and her hazel eye contact and prayed that nothing would go wrong today. "Please," she added.

As the days went by, Twylar found it harder to balance her double life. Her heart ached with loyalty to Willow while her conscience gnawed at her with guilt. It wasn't easy pretending everything was fine with The Legends; the weight of her secret built an invisible wall between her and her friends. Every morning, Twylar put on her disguise, feeling the heavy burden of what might happen if her truth came out. Despite trying to act normal, the fear of someone discovering her secret was always there, like a dark cloud that never left her side.

One afternoon, while she and Willow chatted by the old oak tree, the principal's voice echoed through the courtyard, calling Twylar to her office. Her world seemed to shrink as she walked, the hushed conversations of her classmates fading into the background. It reminded her of her childhood... Soon, Twylar felt herself diving into another memory...

It was Twylar's first day of high school. Her usual guard, Robert Stanley (or as Twylar liked to call him 'Mr. Stanley'), lagged behind as she and her friends walked to school. He was clearly paying much more attention to his phone rather than his duty. Once they had made it to their first class, Twylar felt Mrs Dylts' boring voice drift her off into a world of flying crackers and gummy pizza, and an army of upside-down teapots with ice cream dolloped on top of each one...

"MISS TWYLAR!" yelled Mrs. Dylts suddenly, waking Twylar from her daydream. "The relative clause is in sentence B!" said Twylar, not giving a thought to what she had said. "This is mathematics!" said Mrs Dylts, clearly self-restraining from abusing her vocal cords any longer. "Oh," Twylar slumped down in her seat. She mentally prepared herself for the lecture and got ready to talk back (In the comfort of her own mind) to stop herself from being on the verge of tears.

Mrs Dylts stared into Twylar's soul before launching into what seemed like a yearlong lecture. "I spend all my time teaching you the laws of mathematics so you can lead a better example to your younger siblings in life! You should count yourself lucky that I am a teacher who cares about your learning!" she snapped. "Then don't care about our learning! I've had enough practice of people not caring about me, so I really wouldn't care..." Twylar muttered under her breath. The bell had rung at last, and Twylar raced out the door; lunchtime had come by almost a second later. Twylar couldn't remember much about what she had done in English and History. The seats were all taken, and even if there were some seats left, nobody would want to sit next to Twylar. Suddenly, she recognised the unmistakable figure of Stacey, Sammy and Christie.

Laughing hysterically, Stacey pulled out her phone and began to record. "Ew, why's she laughing like a pig? And everyone says you're the demon around here..." muttered Moon. Twylar turned around and found all her friends were standing behind her. Lily had left her packed lunch on the table beside Christie, who picked it up. "Scrambled eggs? Toast? What, are you that poor Lily?" asked Christie sweetly, still holding onto Lily's Lunch. "Leave her out this..." grumbled Twylar. "Oooooh, coming to get me, are you now, you demon?" mocked Christie.

Stacey laughed, still recording. "Unlike you, demon, Me and Stacey have white hair! Meaning we-" began Christie, "Meaning that I should start calling you grandma? Matches your wrinkles on that big forehead of yours" sneered Twylar. "That we are true heirs to the throne" finished Christie. She had now seemed to take in what Twylar had said. Christie blazed with anger.

She threw the container of scrambled eggs at Twylar, who stumbled to the floor. Her hair is now covered in egg. Christie snatched a tray from a nearby table and dumped the contents on Twylar's head. Unluckily, the scorching tomato soup burned Twylar's scalp, and she fanned it anxiously. It did nothing. Still feeling the pain, Twylar could do nothing but cry. Moon, Lily and Ava were restrained by several other students (all boys, who had fallen in love with Christie) and Sammy. "Hah! That'll teach ya to go biting off more than you could swallow!" Christie stamped her dirty shoe all over Twylar's face. She bent down, smiled menacingly, and began to pull Twylar's hair. She shrieked with pain while Stacey continued to film. She broke out of Christie's grip and took refuge in the girls' bathroom. Soon joined by the rest of her friends.

Twylar hurried herself into a stall and silently cried. "BY ORDER OF THE PRINCESS, LET US IN!" came the demanding voice of Christie from outside the bathroom. "NO, YOU HAIRY PIG!" yelled Lily back, as she used a small chair and box full of soap to barricade the door. Of course, that wasn't enough, so Lily and Ava had to stay against the door. "Twylar?" Moon knocked on the door of Twylar's stall, expecting an answer. Twylar sighed and came out of her hiding place. Her face was tear-stained, and it was clear that the soup, scrambled eggs, and her tears had mixed into one. "Oh Twy..." mumbled Moon. Lily and Ava were still huddled against the door, with the threatening demands of Christie. ("IF YOU DON'T OPEN THIS DOOR, FATHER'LL SACK YOUR STUPID DAD!!" she yelled to Ava.)

Moon looked at her in horror. The tomato soup had mixed with the scrambled eggs, which had marinated in her tears for the last minute.

"Lily, this looks like a job for you... Ava, I'll help with that door!" admitted Moon as she swapped places with Lily. Lily pulled out the shampoo from her bag, and Moon and Ava stared in disbelief. "What? A girl's gotta be prepared..." Lily muttered as she ushered Twylar to sit on a spare chair next to the sink. Lily checked if anyone else was using the stalls before soaking Twylar's hair in the warm school water. Lily doused Twylar's hair in the heavily scented shampoo before soaking her hair in water again.

Lily plugged in her hair dryer and began to dry Twylar's hair. "Thanks... I owe you guys!" smiled Twylar. Moon smiled back. It seemed like the hoard of people had left by now, so it was safe for Ava and Moon to step back. "Sorry, I can't do anything about your shirt..." admitted Lily after stepping back to admire Twylar's hair. It was free of soup and eggs, and it smelled like lavender. "Guys, it's three o'clock already!" realised Ava, swishing her black ponytail. (She hadn't dyed it yet) Careful to avoid any teachers, they managed to sneak out of school. "I wish Willow was still here in the Isle of Irene!" sighed Ava. One by one, all of Twylar's friends had arrived home, leaving Twylar to walk alone and vulnerable to the castle. A little behind her, a black car zoomed past. She could just make out the smug faces of Christie and Stacey. And just Twylar's luck, it had started raining.

The guard who was supposed to be accompanying Twylar had left her behind and was laughing happily with the duo, driving away in the black car. She sighed sadly and allowed the rain to wet her heavily perfumed hair. "Maybe that'll get rid of the smell," thought Twylar, whose lungs couldn't handle the strong lavender smell. Lily had put too much of it on her hair anyway. Once Twylar had made it to the castle, three blurry figures stood in front of the gates. One was bulky and large, the other with what looked like grey wavy hair and the other with straight, short grey hair. Twylar understood who they were. The rain cleared up, and she could see them more clearly now. Sammy smiled menacingly at Twylar.

Since Twylar was all alone, all three of them came charging at Twylar at once. Her hair was being pulled, her skin was being scratched, and punches were being thrown at her face. At the end of it, Twylar was left black and blue. Stacey pulled out her phone and snapped several pictures of a very beaten-up Twylar, sniggering as she put her phone back in her pocket. Stacey and Sammy seemed content with their handiwork, while it was clear Christie had planned more. She pulled on some plastic gloves before digging her hand into the earth. She pulled out a revolting number of worms and threw them at Twylar. She didn't stop there. She dug for more worms while Sammy held Twylar back. She was useless. Why couldn't she defend herself? If she really was a demon, why couldn't she just use her demon abilities to blast them all away? Twylar screwed up her face and did the only thing that she was able to do. She cried. She cried and cried and cried. Christie paused and nudged Stacey to take a picture. Sammy let go of Twylar in bewilderment and laughed hysterically. Taking advantage of this, Twylar ran into the gates straight to the arms of her mother.

Queen Amber shot a furious look at Christie, Stacey, and Sammy before heading to the nurse's wing to check on Twylar's injuries. She carefully picked all the worms out of Twylar's hair and gave her a tight hug. Twylar felt a wave of relief wash over her as she ran into her mother. Amber told her to go to her bedroom and rest. As Twylar made her way upstairs, she could hear her mother shouting angrily and the whimpers of Stacey and Christie.

Once she was lying on her bed, the pain from her bruises and cuts began to fade a bit. Twylar felt a confusing mix of relief at being safe and a deep sadness about her situation. Queen Amber soon joined her, bringing a warm cloth to clean Twylar's face and a soothing balm for her injuries.

"Why didn't you tell me sooner?" Amber asked, her voice reflecting both concern and anger. Twylar looked down, not wanting to make her mother feel any worse.

"I thought I could handle it," she whispered. Amber sighed deeply, brushing a strand of hair from Twylar's forehead.

"This ends now," she declared firmly. "No one messes with my daughter and gets away with it."

Twylar felt comforted by her mother's determination. For the first time in a long while, she believed that things might get better. With her mother's help, Twylar decided she wouldn't let anyone make her feel small again. What a lie that was.

Twylar felt the gaze of what seemed to be a hundred other kids fall upon her as she sat on the small, moth-eaten chair outside the principal's office. She had spent at least half the time she was supposed to wait to remember quite a nasty memory, and now she was wishing that the telling off she knew would happen happened now. The menacing-looking headteacher strutted out of her office and commanded Twylar to enter. She sat down in her office while the headteacher played a CCTV camera recording. It showed a clear image of a girl with straight, long red hair. Willow was hidden by a tree branch covering half of the camera's view. They could see the red-haired girl was painting on the school walls. "Coral, that's you, isn't it?" said the headteacher sweetly before banging her fist on the table. "IT'S YOU, CORAL!" she roared angrily, spit flying from her mouth. The next few moments whizzed by, ending with the headteacher phoning Camilla and expelling Twylar.

Twylar hung her head low in shame. Why had she listened to Willow? Surely, if your friends get you in trouble, they're not actually your friends? Oh, she was so stupid! She let her feelings towards Willow control her, fearing that if she didn't do what Willow said, she would lose her best friend all over again. Now look where it landed her. She kept her head low, not daring to look at the bewildered faces of her friends and the worried face of Willow. She caught up with Twylar just before she left the school gates, "Hey, did I get in trouble too?" she asked, her voice shaky. "Oh, no," said Twylar, surprised to find Willow relieved at her words. It was like she didn't even care that Twylar had gotten expelled! Twylar smiled nervously at Willow and watched her run happily to her other friends. Twylar sighed and stepped out of the school gates. On her way to the cave she called home, a small boy crouched at the end of the wooden pier, drinking the river water with small, cupped hands.

 Suddenly, the little boy began to cough uncontrollably. He gasped for air, alerting his older brother. Twylar looked on in horror. She rushed to him, "Is there anything I can do?" she asked, watching as the older brother pressed on the boy's stomach. "Yes, mam, go get some hospital folk!" he called out as Twylar rushed to the nearest hospital. By the time she and the doctors had come back, the boy was facing near death. They carried him and placed him at the back of their ambulance. The older brother sat beside his younger brother. Twylar replayed the gruesome scene over and over in her head that night and refused to speak or explain to anyone what had happened at school that day.

At the crack of dawn, Twylar woke early. She did not go back to sleep until she saw that Camilla had woken up, she didn't want to explain to her great-aunt either. She couldn't stay quiet, though. She needed to talk. So, she went to the only person she could comfortably talk with. "Estella?" asked Twylar,

"Yes?" she replied, tying her curly light pink hair.

"Can we go outside and talk?" whispered Twylar, relieved to see Estella nodding.

They walked outside the cave, feeling a wave of cold rush over the two of them. With a heavy heart, Twylar explained everything. Estella nodded and waited for Twylar to finish before talking to herself. "I'm glad you shared this with me. Now, you don't have to lift the burden alone!" Estella smiled, "I won't tell anyone unless you tell me to." she said firmly. Twylar smiled back. She was glad to have a friend like Estella! "You look like you need a hug!" grinned Estella as she pulled Twylar into a bear hug. After that, Twylar began being herself again (well, not with her appearance; she was still the red-haired Coral that had been expelled a day ago). She was talking to everyone animatedly, staying up all night with her friends and eating dinner with everyone else. The yellow flames lit up Twylar's ecstatic expression, and she began sharing jokes Moon had once told her. The next day, all the residents of Mai 'ho were ordered to meet at the Centre of the village. Twylar and her friends were at the front of the crowd, wondering why a short, squat little man with a roll of parchment was standing before them all on a stool.

"RESIDENTS OF MAI'HO," he began. "THE TWO SCHOOLS OF THIS VILLAGE ARE HEREBY CLOSED UNTIL FURTHER NOTICE. WATER WILL BE SUPPLIED TO EVERYONE; DO NOT DRINK FROM THE RIVER WE SETTLE UPON!" he declared, "IT HAS BEEN POISONED, SO WE HAVE FOUND OUT FROM UNFORTUNATE MR GREGORY!" he continued. Twylar looked behind her and saw the older brother she had seen before. A tall woman stood next to him, her ears all blotchy from crying. "MAI'HO HAS BEEN TAKEN OVER BY THE BLACK ANGEL, THE COUNCIL OF MAI'HO ARE THEREFORE POWERLESS AND WE PLEAD THAT YOU KEEP OUT HIS WAY-" Twylar cast a confusing look at the short man. The Black Angel? Why was everyone so scared when he had said his name? "Ale- Jack!" Twylar whispered to a very grumpy looking Alex. He had been in that mood ever since he was forced to wear his black spiky wig and neck collar. "What?" he whispered back, "Who's the Black Angel?" she answered. Alex shivered from fear, "He- he's a guy... they say he's called the Black Angel because of his power, like a good force for evil..."

Alex whimpered. Twylar urged him to continue, "He's ruthless, Twy, would kill even a baby if it got in his way", Alex shuddered. Twylar looked at him in surprise. "THE COUNCIL HAS YOUR SAFETY AT HEART, WE ADVISE YOU COMPLETE YOUR SHOPPING TODAY AS THE BLACK ANGEL AND HIS FORCES ARE ARRIVING TOMORROW!" the short man finished with a bow, day people crowded the markets, all toppling over themselves to buy what they needed. Camilla, however, wasn't one of them. "Excuse me!" she said, in a honey-sweet voice exactly like Twylar's mother. The man at the counter stared at her in surprise. "Oh, please, the name's Amber," she winked at him. "Just... a loaf of bread, or... if you were so kind..." Camilla paused. "Have 10! Free of charges!" said the man, his voice misty as though his soul was in another world, but he had left his body back on earth. "Oh!" exclaimed Camilla, with a tone of mock surprise. "Well, I'd also like some tinned soup, a carton of milk, oh and... I'm a *single* mother..." added Camilla. They walked home that day with a supply of food and water that would last them well over three months!

The next day, Twylar decided to go outside for fresh air. She wasn't too concerned about the Black Angel. If she saw him, she would simply pause time and walk back to the cave. But the problem was, she didn't. A small boy around the age of the unfortunate Gregory. He lay shivering on the white pebbly floor of the playground, with the slide crushed to dust. She immediately understood who the man towering over the boy was- the Black Angel. A hero in the face of evil, with powers supposedly so corrupted, it would make the strongest man alive shiver in fear. Twylar didn't have time to think. She swiftly pushed the boy out of harm's way and allowed the Black Angel's punch to hit her instead. The young boy ran far from the playground, not daring to look back. The Black Angel shot a look of venom at Twylar, who was still disguised as Coral. She had saved his prey.

The Black Angel's cold eyes scanned Twylar down as though to check she was worthy of his time. His neat, dark brown hair lay styled on top of his head, his square glasses reflecting the sun. He readjusted his black tie and pushed up his glasses. He was wearing a smart black suit with a white shirt underneath, with shiny black shoes to match. "Who are you?" he purred, his voice calm. Twylar paused to think, "Coral" she snorted back. The Black Angel smiled a toothy grin full of sharp, pure white teeth. The weapon he was wielding, a stick with sharp blades at both ends of it, glinted in the sunlight.

Twylar was by herself. No one to help her. He charged at Twylar, who dodged so that she received a mere cut on her cheek. She couldn't reveal her true identity-not now. So, she tried punching as Coral. She swung her fists at the Black Angel, who dodged as though she were nothing. His blade cut a piece of her red wig, giving her quite a nasty haircut. Twylar knew she wouldn't last as long as Coral. She ripped off her wig, freeing her hair from its prison. She didn't have time to rip off the face mask, though, as the Black angel did it for her. She received a bloody nose, one cut on her cheek and a cut under her chin. The face mask fell to the floor, and Twylar winced as the pain became stronger. He was too fast...

She received more and more cuts, barely having any time to dodge. By the end of it, she could barely stand.

She tried throwing a punch, but her fists didn't listen.

Twylar's vision blurred as the Black Angel's attacks continued with relentless fury. She could feel the weight of exhaustion pressing down on her, yet a stubborn resolve kept her on her feet. Drawing on the last reserves of her strength, she summoned a burst of energy, capturing a fleeting moment of surprise on the Black Angel's face. Her body moved almost instinctively, weaving through his strikes with newfound agility. As the battle raged on, an unexpected sense of clarity washed over her— she was fighting not just for herself but for everyone who had suffered at the hands of this merciless villain. The sounds of the village, the faces of her friends, and the memory of her mother's determination fueled her resolve. In a final, desperate manoeuvre, Twylar managed to disarm the Black Angel, sending his weapon clattering to the ground. He simply smiled. Twylar watched in shock as the weapon flew back into his hand. She could barely stand, yet she hadn't even laid a single scratch on him. She now understood why he was called the Black Angel.

Twylar couldn't fight anymore. Her muscles screamed in agony as she fell to her knees, bruised and battered. Her spirit, however, remained unbroken, fuelled by a fierce determination. She wanted to get up again and continue the battle, but her body refused to obey, every limb heavy with exhaustion. She lay on the ground, feeling the cold, pebbly soil pressing against her skin, sending shivers through her battered frame.

Through the haze of pain, she caught a glimpse of the Black Angel, his sinister grin stretching from ear to ear, a haunting mockery of her struggle. The world around her started to blur, the sounds of the battlefield fading into a distant echo. She felt herself slowly blacking out, the edges of her vision darkening.

As her consciousness slipped away, she clung to the memory of her mother's unwavering determination, the strength she always saw in her eyes. She also thought of her friends, their faces flashing before her, each one a beacon of hope and camaraderie. She vowed that this wouldn't be the end, even as darkness began to engulf her. Twylar's spirit was a flame that could not be extinguished, even as her body lay still on the battlefield.

Yet, even in the darkness, a glimmer of strength remained within Twylar. As she lay on the cold ground, the memory of her mother's unwavering determination surged through her veins like a comforting elixir, reigniting the fire within. She felt a warmth spreading through her chest, a vivid reminder that her spirit could never be extinguished. Her friends, her mother's legacy, and the village of Mai'ho were not just fleeting memories—they were her driving force.

Drawing from the well of resilience she had yet to fully tap into, Twylar's resolve solidified into an unbreakable promise: she would rise again, not only for herself but for the hope she harboured for a brighter future. She remembered the evenings spent under the starlit sky, listening to her mother's tales of valour and perseverance. Those stories were now her fuel, each word a spark that set her resolve ablaze.

The Black Angel's cruel laughter echoed in the recesses of her mind, but she knew this was not her end—merely the beginning of a new chapter, one in which she would emerge stronger and more determined than ever before. She envisioned herself standing tall, her eyes reflecting the indomitable spirit of her ancestors, her heart beating with the rhythm of their collective strength.

Her spirit, though momentarily subdued, blazed like a beacon that would guide her through the darkest of times. It was a promise of resilience that would one day see her vanquish the shadows that sought to consume her. She willed for any part of her body to move; she would even be content for just a finger to wiggle. But it didn't. The horrified gasps of villagers clouded Twylar's ears. They didn't dare move a step closer. She had blacked out completely. But when she opened her eyes again, she found herself in a familiar place. The white void. She saw her mother emerge from the white mist surrounding them, and a warm smile greeted her. Queen Amber planted a kiss on Twylar's forehead, and suddenly, Twylar found all her injuries had been healed. Queen Amber smiled again before walking into the white mist.

Twylar awoke again to find the Black Angel towering above her, she tried to stand up, but she found she couldn't...

The screams and shouts from the crowd told Twylar that she didn't look the same as before, and she was right. She had become a light amethyst. Her blonde and yellow hair swished in the wind. Suddenly, the voice of her mother rang crisp and clear through her mind- "I'm controlling your body, sweetie, leave it to me", reassured Queen Amber. Twylar let her mother settle things for her. She watched as Queen Amber stood up and brushed the dirt off her clothes.

Furious that 'Twylar' had been able to stand up, he charged relentlessly again. This time, he managed to cut off her whole arm. Twylar stared horrified at the small lump of what used to be her shoulder. The villagers looked away. Though Queen Amber merely sighed. Within seconds, her arm had regenerated, ending with golden light escaping from her new fingertips. "Thought you'd do better," Queen Amber sighed. She sounded like herself, calm and undoubtedly with a plan in mind. "Black Angel this, Black Angel that, you're nothing but a heartless monster rampaging for utterly no reason." Twylar understood what her mother was trying to do. If she had enraged the Black Angel, he wouldn't be using his head to defeat Queen Amber. He would be acting on his emotions! That would give Queen Amber the upper hand! "I should take notes..." wondered Twylar. She started from her mother's point of view, the way she was fighting...

It reminded her of- "Eleanor's dance!" he gasped. "Eleanor's dance?" wondered Twylar. Her mother's fighting style did replicate a dance, she slid across the white pebbly floor and landed a punch on the Black Angel. He grinned, baring his sharp teeth. A plethora of ghostly pale dogs rose from the ground. They charged at Queen Amber. They bit into her, leaving deep wounds on her skin. "Now it's my turn," Queen Amber purred. Golden light shone from her wounds, and within seconds, they were healed.

 The Black Angel's rage grew with each failed attempt to overpower Queen Amber, his attacks becoming increasingly frenzied and uncoordinated. With every move, Queen Amber's graceful yet powerful counterattacks mirrored the elegance of a well-choreographed dance, her body moving fluidly as if guided by an unseen rhythm. The villagers watched in fear, their hearts pounding as the battle unfolded before their eyes. Despite the Black Angel's relentless onslaught, Queen Amber remained a beacon of resilience and hope, her golden light illuminating the darkened battlefield. The ground beneath them seemed to tremble with the intensity of their clash, a testament to the enormous power they wielded. The air crackled with energy, and for a moment, it seemed as though time itself stood still, holding its breath in anticipation of the outcome. Twylar, now a silent observer within her own body, marvelled at her mother's strength.

Her healing abilities were beyond her own. She didn't even have that golden light when she was healing herself!

Queen Amber was arguably faster than the Black Angel, as fast as the speed of light. Suddenly, she paused and jumped back as the Black Angel's blade almost cut her in half. He grinned menacingly. The playground was destroyed at this point, a hole where the seesaw used to stand. Queen Amber sighed and held her hands out. A small, gold thread formed between her fingers; she stretched it out so it became even more thinner. The Black Angel stared at the small, golden thread. Twylar could feel it was as soft as the clouds; she could feel her mother's calm conception. She positioned the thread like a bow, and when she let go, at least 40 yellow flames charged towards the Black Angel from the golden bow. They hit him, leaving him unconscious on the floor. Queen Amber had done it. Suddenly, the Black Angel's body was surrounded by a strong wind; it dispersed, and they could see he was no longer there.

Chapter Eleven

Twylar found she could control her body again—she was no longer a light amethyst. The sea of villagers surrounded her, all applauding her mixed with screams and shouts of delight.

Twylar, feeling an overwhelming rush of relief and gratitude, stood amidst the jubilant villagers, their expressions of admiration and joy a stark contrast to the fierce battle that had just transpired. As the echoes of their applause filled the air, she raised her hand to silence them, her voice steady yet filled with emotion. "You don't have to be afraid of the Black Angel anymore!" she declared, her eyes sweeping over the crowd. For a moment, the chaos and destruction of the battlefield seemed distant, replaced by a profound sense of exultation. Gasping for breath, Twylar looked around the crowd. Some of her schoolmates were here too, even the headteacher! They were at the front of the crowd. They looked at Twylar in awe. Of course, they didn't realise she was Coral— she hadn't removed her wig in front of them. Along with the playground, Twylar's wig and eye contacts lay as a small pile of ash; they drifted away in the wind. Now, Twylar was not the only one who had just finished a battle.

"AVA!" shouted Lily. Zilas stared nervously at the three tall, hooded men. One of them stood on the wooden pier. (Mai'ho is surrounded by a lake, so they have piers at the borders) Ava lay in a crumpled heap at the foot of one of the hooded men, "Go", it said in a throaty voice. "Find the sceptre!" he commanded, his voice inhumane. Zilas shivered. "Lily... they're after the Demon lord's sceptre!" he realised. The other hooded man nodded, sped away from the pier and left the two to his comrade. "Now, I'm not letting you chase after him..." He had finally acknowledged that they were there. Zilas quickly formed the faint, globe-like shield around him and Lily, protecting them from their opponent's attacks. "You're quite funny... y'know?" he rasped. "He gave me this power... I must not disappoint," he held his hands in front of his face. He lowered his hood. What Lily and Zilas saw would haunt last their nightmares for the rest of their days.

He had no eyes. His snake-like mouth curved into a wicked grin, and his pointy nose outlined the faint, bumpy-looking skin of where his eyes should be. "I was born... infected," he began. Zilas turned to look at Lily, and she turned to look at him. "If he starts explaining about his life or something, it'll give us an opening!" she whispered to Zilas. He nodded. "What do you mean, infected?" asked Zilas, trying to steer him into a long explanation. "I was born in Gale, one of the poorest villages here in Volcano Hills," he explained. "A curse... was put on me... to protect the lives of everyone in Volcano Hills..." he clenched his fists angrily, but he spoke calmly. "I was given the curse of the black rose. If not passed on to another host once the previous one has died, it puts the world at great risk." he eyed Zilas, who was trying to undo the barrier while he was talking. "But... payment must be made... to bear the burden..." he felt his bumpy skin where his eyes should have been. "They took my eyes," he said plainly. "Now, the curse of the black rose lends me great strength, but for payment," he pulled on his brown hair, and it came off lightly. It revealed very knobbly skin; he was eyeless and bald. "This was the last time I used the black rose's power. I was weak without it, a mere vessel. But I could not wield it..." Zilas had done it. He had led Lily out for a sneak attack while staying in the barrier himself.

The man took no notice of Lily and blocked her attack. She lay crumpled on the ground right next to Ava. Zilas stared in horror. "But then he..." the man continued, "He gave me his own... yes, enough talking... I must not disappoint..." he murmured to himself. He walked up to Zilas' barrier, put his arm through it and walked straight in. "I cannot touch you in here, very strong magic indeed, whereas in average cases I would have succeeded." his raspy voice sent chills down Zilas' spine. A prickly, spidery-like sensation coursed through his body. "Wha- what is this?" demanded Zilas, feeling himself losing consciousness. "It's the power... *he* gave me..." he answered. He nodded, "The Black Angel is indeed the hero of all evil..." his cruel smile turned into a nefarious grin.

Zilas felt the darkness creeping in, an unsettling numbness spreading from his limbs to his core as the eyeless man's grip tightened around his consciousness. His vision began to blur, the forms of Lily and Ava fading into the eerie mist that enveloped the pier. The man's voice, still raspy and malevolent, echoed faintly in his ears as if coming from a distance. Desperation surged within Zilas as he struggled to stand up.

With immense effort, a faint glimmer of resistance sparked within him, and with every ounce of willpower, he managed to whisper an incantation. The spell surged through his veins, breaking the man's hold for a fleeting moment. It was the spell he had learned from an old book he had stolen; he was in the golden age of his thievery, and he read the curly, loopy writing of the ancient spell book. In that brief respite, Zilas saw an opening and, mustering the last of his magical and mental strength, unleashed a powerful surge of energy that struck the man, reeling back with a howl of rage.

The force of the attack shattered the oppressive barrier that had surrounded them. Zilas collapsed to his knees, gasping for breath, his vision darkening once more. He succumbed to the unconsciousness; he caught a final glimpse of Lily. She was rising to her feet, determination blazing in her eyes. Ava had gotten up, too. "Guys!" Zilas breathed.

As Zilas' consciousness waned, his vision blurred, and his strength ebbed away, Lily and Ava, summoning every ounce of their velour, confronted the eyeless adversary with unflinching determination. The eyeless man's presence was a chilling void. Yet, each strike they delivered, synchronised and precise, pushed him further back, their resolve a force so formidable that even the darkest of curses could not extinguish it. The air around them crackled with energy, a blend of Zilas' lingering spell and their own fierce magic, creating an electrifying atmosphere that pulsed with their combined might.

In a final, dazzling burst of light, they unleashed a torrent of power that enveloped the eyeless man. He staggered back in surprise.

He simply wiped away the energy wrapping around him as though trying to squeeze him to death. "I'm an elite member of the Fireheavens, the Black Angel's servants. We obey every word he speaks. Such silly incantations or such weak, silly little spells won't work on me," he revealed. "But... you can't see! How're you this-" Lily demanded. "It is... his power," from behind the man came a very large, single eyeball. "This is his... lending it to a mere, dirty servant... I would never, but for the sake of him, I shall accept his power..." he muttered. The eyeball grew fierce as though fire were in its eyes. Suddenly, weapons of all sizes appeared, suspended in the air behind the man. Zilas quickly set up the barrier.

The eyeless man laughed, "Very strong barrier, boy, but such strong magic means you won't be able to hold on long..." the man continued laughing. The weapons, after throwing themselves at the barrier, picked themselves up to do it again. The man was right, Zilas couldn't hold on any longer. They could see from the barrier that a particularly large, sharp weapon that resembled the Black Angel's double blade was fixed on Zilas, hitting the barrier continuously. Zilas held his hands to his ears, trying to stop the flood of sounds reaching his eardrums. "COVER YOUR EARS!" he shouted to Lily and Ava, "THE SOUND HAS SOMETHING TO DO WITH IT!" Lily and Ava nodded and covered their ears, too. "You've figured me out," said the man calmly. "But covering your ears with your hands is not enough-" Suddenly, he was lying on the ground. The weapons had stopped attacking, but the eye was still there. It turned around to face- "Camilla!" yelled Ava. Zilas undid the barrier; they were free to jump into Camilla's arms. "Guess I was a little late..." she joked as she saw the conditions of the three. "Well, you did an amazing job holding out on your own!" they beamed. But their troubles were not over yet. The eyeless man stood up, this time with more difficulty. "Ah, Camilla, so the rumours are true then, I assume?" his tone was casual, as though meeting up with an old friend. "Yes, indeed they are, Robbie!" Camilla smiled back.

"Please, you flatter me, call me by my name. Thank you," he purred.

"Alright then, Robert, how's life going?" she asked, standing in front of Lily, Ava and Zilas.

"Amazing, absolutely extraordinary, really," the eyeless man focused his floating eye on Camilla. She did not look like Queen Amber anymore; she had her normal straight black hair and serpent-green eyes.

Camilla's eyes narrowed as she faced Robert, her confident stance unwavering. "Extraordinary, you say?" she mused, her voice calm yet laced with a hint of menace. "It seems we have unfinished business, Robert." The air around them grew tense, the weight of their shared history palpable. Zilas, Lily, and Ava watched in awe, their trust in Camilla's strength unwavering. With a swift, fluid motion, Camilla conjured an intricate spell, her hands weaving an ethereal pattern in the air. The power emanating from her was immense, a testament to her mastery of magic.

Camilla took a deep breath before raising her hands above her head. She quickly pulled them down, and from her hand was an overflowing surge of power. You could visibly see it pour from Camilla's hand onto the floor. She smiled again. "Robert, you do know your boss was taken down earlier today, yes?" Robert's face showed no emotion, but without his boss, what were they supposed to do? "By whom?" he inquired. "My niece, *amazing* raw strength she has!" Camilla paused to admire the look on Robert's face. Even if he had no eyes or eyebrows, the way his mouth was shaped said it all. "And... how old is she?" he said through gritted teeth. "If the Black Angel was defeated by a mere 15-year-old, Camilla's niece must be very skilled indeed..." he thought.

Camilla beamed, "15!" she answered. Even though Robert didn't look aghast by this statement, Camilla could clearly tell he was.

Camilla's expression changed; she remained confident. "Robert, it's over. The era of the Black Angel is ending, and a new dawn is upon us, hopefully, people have invented self-cleaning mops for houses by now!" she declared, her voice echoing with finality. Robert's expression, though eyeless, conveyed a mixture of disbelief and annoyance. It was clear these two had a history together.

Suddenly, the ground trembled beneath their feet, and a fissure opened, releasing a blinding light that enveloped Robert. He struggled against the pulling force, his form flickering as though caught between worlds. Camilla exchanged a mischievous look before clapping her hands together. Suddenly, Robert's whole body was engulfed by black flames. A shadowy portal opened beneath him, and out came a pale white arm. It dragged him into the contents of the shadows, the last of him trying to find something to grab onto. "Dark wingless tactics, did you forget?" Camilla smiled.

The silence that followed was profound; the air cleared of dark magic. Zilas, Lily, and Ava rushed to Camilla's side, their expressions a mix of relief and admiration. "You did it, Camilla," Ava breathed, her eyes shining with gratitude.

Camilla smiled warmly at them, the severity of the battle giving way to a rare moment of tenderness. "Of course I did! I'm such an icon~" she beamed.

As they stood there, united in victory, the first rays of dawn broke over the horizon, casting a golden glow over the battlefield. But the battle was not over not yet. "Where's Twy and the others?" asked Ava, "Out where the playground is- no, uh, used to be... heh," Camilla pointed north. "What happened to the playground?" asked Zilas, "Destroyed! But I don't think we have to pay for it... right?" Ava groaned. They had spent all their last few pennies on food on water; they wouldn't have enough to pay for a playground!

Once they arrived, they could barely see Twylar as she was being congratulated by swarms of ecstatic villagers, each either rewarding her with a pat on the shoulder or the village kids imitating her (Queen Amber's) fighting moves amongst themselves. They didn't seem to care about her hair or hair eyes!

Camilla, Zilas, Ava, and Lily approached the gathering, their steps light but purposeful. The villagers made way for them, their faces glowing with admiration and gratitude. Twylar looked up from the crowd, her eyes meeting Camilla's, and a smile spread across her face.

"You did well, Twy, almost as good as me! But not quite-" Camilla said, her voice carrying both praise and pride. "The Black Angel's defeat marks the beginning of our new journey."

Twylar nodded, her expression serious. "What about the Demon Lord's sceptre?"

As the group conversed, the villagers began to disperse, returning to their daily routines with renewed hope. The sun climbed higher into the welcome arms of the sky, bathing the village in warmth and light.

"Let's regroup and plan our next steps," Camilla suggested. "It's most likely hidden in either a building or mountain if Queen Amber was the one that hid it." The Legends made their way to the village hall, a modest yet sturdy building that had miraculously survived the recent turmoil. Inside, they gathered around a large wooden table, maps and documents spread out before them.

"We need to fortify our defences," Zilas began, tracing a finger along the perimeter of the village on the map. "And we should send scouts to monitor any unusual activity in the surrounding areas."

Ava nodded in agreement. "I'll organise a team to start rebuilding the playground and other damaged structures. We can't afford to lose the morale we've worked so hard to restore."

Lily chimed in, her voice steady and determined. "I'll gather the healers to tend to the injured and ensure everyone is in good health. We don't know if the king has found out the sceptre's location."

Camilla looked around the table, her heart swelling with pride. They were all like her children. She cared for them as if they were really all her children.

As the meeting adjourned, the group dispersed to carry out their respective duties. Camilla stepped outside, her eyes drifting to the horizon where the first signs of hope glinting across the lake. They'd make sure the Cursed Blue wouldn't be able to grow- never again!

It had been a couple of days since their last meeting, and an uneasy feeling gnawed at Twylar. The uncertainty was unbearable. Driven by a restless need to find answers, she decided to sneak out under the cover of night. The moon hung low, casting an eerie glow over the sleeping village. Shadows stretched across the ground like fingers of darkness, and she moved silently, her footsteps barely a whisper against the cold, dew-laden earth.

Unbeknownst to her, Alex had sensed her unease and was quietly trailing her, ensuring she wouldn't face any danger alone. His presence was almost spectral, blending seamlessly with the night. As they ventured deeper into the woods, a chilling stillness surrounded them. The trees loomed like silent sentinels, their gnarled branches intertwining to form a canopy that blocked out the moonlight. Shadows danced and flickered, creating ghostly shapes that seemed to move with a life of their own.

The air was thick with the damp, earthy scent of moss and decaying leaves, a stark contrast to the crisp, clear night. The occasional hoot of an owl echoed through the stillness and the rustling of unseen creatures added to the eerie atmosphere. Twylar felt a shiver run down her spine, but her resolve remained unshaken. They had to find the Demon Lord's sceptre before it was too late.

As they pressed on, the sound of soft footsteps behind them went unnoticed. Willow, hidden in the shadows, followed stealthily, her face a mask of determination. She was unwilling to let her friends face the danger alone, though Alex and Twylar remained oblivious to her presence. Her heart pounded in her chest as she kept pace, her breath coming in quiet, measured intervals.

Together, the three of them forged ahead, their path illuminated only by the faint light of the stars. The forest seemed to close in around them, the trees whispering secrets they couldn't quite understand. Every step brought them closer to Mount Mai, where they believed the sceptre was hidden. The journey was fraught with uncertainty, but their bond and shared purpose gave them strength.

Midnight approached as they neared the base of the mountain. The air grew colder, and an unsettling feeling settled over them. The path ahead was steep and treacherous, with loose rocks and dense underbrush threatening to impede their progress. But they knew they had to press on. The fate of their world depended on it. With a final glance at each other, they began their ascent, ready to face whatever challenges lay ahead. The silence was broken only by the distant howl of a wolf, a haunting reminder of the peril that lurked in every shadow.

As they climbed, the incline grew steeper, demanding every ounce of their courage to be summoned. Twylar glanced up at the towering peak, its ominous silhouette outlined against the starlit sky. She could feel the weight of their mission pressing down on her shoulders, but she drew courage from the resolve etched on Alex's face and the silent support she knew Willow provided from the shadows.

Unexpectedly, a faint glow appeared ahead, a flicker of light piercing the dark expanse of the forest. They exchanged wary glances and moved cautiously toward it, their footsteps deliberate and silent. The glow grew stronger, revealing the entrance to a hidden cave, partially obscured by overgrown vines and ancient stone.

Twylar's heart raced as she reached out to push aside the foliage, revealing the rough-hewn entrance. The light emanated from within, casting long shadows that danced eerily on the cave walls. Her breath caught in her throat as she stepped inside, Alex and Willow close behind her, their presence a comforting reminder that she was not alone.

Inside the cave, the air was cool and damp, a stark contrast to the chill of the mountainside. The light source came from an enchanted torch, its flames flickering with an otherworldly luminescence. They followed the winding path, the torchlight guiding their way deeper into the heart of the mountain.

As they ventured further, the stillness of the cave was interrupted by an almost imperceptible hum, growing louder with each step. Twylar's pulse quickened as they rounded a bend and came face to face with a massive stone door intricately carved with ancient runes and symbols. The first stage is to get through to the sceptre.

As they approached the massive stone door, the air grew thick with anticipation. Twylar steeled herself, feeling the reassuring presence of Alex by her side and the unseen support of Willow lurking in the shadows. She reached out, tracing her fingers over the ancient runes, feeling a faint vibration beneath her touch. With a deep breath, she pushed the door open, revealing a large, dimly lit chamber beyond.

Willow crept silently behind them, her senses on high alert. The room was vast, with stalactites hanging precariously from the ceiling and a faint glimmer of treasure in the far corners. The walls were adorned with old frescoes depicting mythical battles and forgotten legends, giving the room an aura of ancient power. Their attention, however, was immediately drawn to the centre of the room, where a massive troll with grey, bumpy skin and a single eye stood guarding a pedestal. The troll's eye narrowed with fury, and it let out an ear-splitting roar, shaking the very ground beneath their feet.

The troll charged at Twylar and Alex with terrifying speed, its heavy footsteps echoing off the chamber walls. Twylar's reflexes kicked in, and she swiftly dodged to the side, summoning her inner fire. With a determined cry, she unleashed a torrent of golden flames at the beast. The troll shrieked in agony as the hot, burning yellow fire engulfed it, but its rage only intensified. It turned its sights back on Twylar, its single eye gleaming with a vengeance.

Alex, never one to falter, saw his opportunity. As the troll lunged towards Twylar, he unsheathed his weapon—a blade forged with enchantments meant to subdue such creatures. The sword's surface shimmered with a blue glow, resonating with the magical energy within. With precise skill, Alex aimed for the troll's exposed flank, driving the weapon deep into its hide. The troll let out a final, thunderous roar before collapsing to the ground, unconscious.

They stood in the aftermath, the room echoing with the troll's last cries. Twylar's flames flickered out, and she rushed to Alex's side, checking for injuries. Willow, who took one scared look at the unconscious troll, shrieked and sped far away from the mountain. She had dropped her phone. As Twylar picked it up, she found it was recording. "She trying to use us for views?" She thought angrily. She stopped the video and deleted it.

With the troll defeated and the chamber now quiet, Twylar and Alex took a moment to recover their breath. The pedestal, now unguarded, revealed a hidden passage that seemed to spiral further into the mountain's depths, beckoning them towards the next stage of their quest.

"Ready?" Alex asked, his eyes reflecting both determination and a hint of exhaustion from the recent battle.

Twylar nodded, stepping forward with renewed resolve. Their journey deeper into the passage was marked by an increasing chill, the air growing colder with every step. The narrow corridor soon widened into a vast ice cavern, its walls glistening with frost and icicles hanging like crystalline daggers from the ceiling. The floor beneath them crunched with each step as they pressed forward.

As they ventured into the cavern, a chilling wind swept through, carrying with it a flurry of snowflakes that danced in the torchlight. Twylar's breath turned to mist as she exhaled, and Alex tightened his grip on his weapon, sensing the presence of another formidable foe lurking within the icy expanse.

Suddenly, a deafening roar echoed through the cavern, reverberating off the walls and sending shivers down their spines. From the shadows emerged an Iceflame dragon, its massive form dominating the icy landscape. The dragon's scales gleamed white against the frosty backdrop, and its teeth were sharp and pointed like icicles. The beast's eyes glowed with a cold, fierce intelligence as it regarded the intruders with a predatory gaze.

Without warning, the dragon unleashed a powerful snowstorm, the sheer force of it barrelling towards Alex like a relentless blizzard. He rolled to the side, narrowly avoiding the brunt of the icy blast. The snow and ice swirled around him, momentarily obscuring his vision.

Twylar, summoning her inner fire once more, melted the incoming snow with a fierce burst of golden flames. The heat from her fire clashed with the cold of the snowstorm, creating a dense steam that momentarily cloaked the battlefield. But the dragon was relentless, not giving them a moment to catch their breath. It shot shards of hard crystal ice towards Twylar with deadly accuracy, forcing her to dodge and weave to avoid the lethal projectiles.

The dragon roared again, its breath creating another blizzard that it hurled directly at Twylar. She countered with a wave of fire, the intense heat colliding with the freezing cold in a spectacular display of elemental forces. The cavern filled with a whirlwind of steam and frost, the air thick with the clash of their powers.

Alex, seizing the opportunity, saw an opening and charged at the dragon, his enchanted blade ready to strike. The dragon turned its icy gaze on him, preparing to unleash another frosty barrage. The ground trembled beneath its massive feet as it shifted to face him, its scales shimmering with an unearthly light.

"Now, Twylar!" he shouted, his voice cutting through the chaos as he aimed to distract the creature long enough for her to find a weakness. His blade, glowing with enchantments, struck the dragon's flank, but its thick scales repelled his initial strike.

Twylar focused her energy, drawing deeper on her well of inner fire. But… she was too cold… The way the Ice flame's attacks seeped into her skin… penetrating her insides with a brutal snowstorm like the hatred inside the one they were facing.

Alex, seizing the opportunity, saw an opening and charged at the dragon, his enchanted blade ready to strike. The dragon turned its icy gaze on him, preparing to unleash another frosty barrage. The ground trembled beneath its massive feet as it shifted to face him, its scales shimmering with an unearthly light.

"Now, Twylar!" he shouted, his voice cutting through the chaos as he aimed to distract the creature long enough for her to find a weakness. His blade, glowing with enchantments, struck the dragon's flank, but its thick scales repelled his initial strike.

Twylar focused her energy, drawing deeper on her well of inner fire. But... she was too cold... The way the Ice flame's attacks seeped into her skin... penetrating her insides with a brutal snowstorm like the hatred inside the one they were facing.

The Iceflame dragon turned its attention back to Twylar, its eyes narrowing as it prepared to launch another assault. Sensing the imminent danger, Alex leapt onto the dragon's back, grasping its scales with all his might. The dragon bucked and twisted, trying to shake him off, but Alex held firm, using his enchanted blade to gain purchase.

With a surge of determination, he managed to reach the dragon's neck, where he found a small, vulnerable spot. Pressing his blade against it, he whispered an incantation and a calming energy radiated from the sword. The dragon's thrashing began to subside, its fierce eyes softening as it gradually succumbed to Alex's influence.

"Twylar, get on its back!" Alex called, his voice steady despite the adrenaline coursing through him. Twylar, with a renewed sense of purpose, climbed onto the dragon, and together, they urged the creature to soar through the cavern, bypassing the remaining obstacles on their path.

As they emerged from the cavern and ascended the mountain, the cold wind whipped around them, but the dragon's presence provided a shield against the elements. They flew higher and higher, the icy peaks of the mountain shimmering below them. The dragon's powerful wings beat rhythmically, carrying them swiftly to their destination.

The mountain's landscape was a mix of jagged cliffs and snow-covered slopes, with occasional patches of hardy, frost-kissed flora clinging to life. The sky above was a deep indigo, dotted with twinkling stars that cast a faint, ethereal glow over the frozen land.

Finally, they reached the summit, where they beheld the Demon Lord's sceptre, encased in a bullet-proof glass shield and guarded by an army of massive toads. The creatures, with their bulging eyes and slimy skin, croaked menacingly as they noticed the intruders.

One of the toads lunged at Alex, its sharp teeth snapping dangerously close to his leg. In response, the Iceflame dragon unleashed a torrent of icy breath, freezing the toad in its tracks and sending the other amphibious defenders scattering in terror. The dragon's ferocity was unmatched, its instincts driving it to protect its newfound allies.

Amid the chaos, Twylar summoned black chains from the depths of her power, directing them towards the glass enclosure. The chains, forged from her dark magic, wrapped around the shield, their dark energy pulsating as they strained against the barrier. The air crackled with energy as the chains tightened, the glass beginning to creak under the pressure.

With a final surge of effort, Twylar focused her magic, the chains tightening and cracking the glass. The echoes of the breaking barrier resonated across the mountaintop, signalling the impending showdown with the ultimate source of their strife. The sceptre, now within reach, glowed ominously, its power a dark force which Twylar knew must never get into the wrong hands.

Twylar found every inch of her body screaming for at least an hour of sleep. Reluctantly, she climbed onto the back of the Iceflame. The wind rushed past her ears, and both Alex and Twylar were covered in various injuries and bruises; they wanted nothing more than a good night's rest.

They made it to the cave, but the worried faces of The Legends welcomed them to what they knew would be either a lecture or a wave of unnecessary questions. "Hey, he's cute- right?" Alex indicated towards the Iceflame. "I'll call him... Frostbite!" announced Alex, ignoring the sunken face of Camilla. "We're... keeping him?" paused Camilla, "Oh come on Camilla! He's really cute!" whined Alex in a last-minute attempt to change her mind. She moaned miserably before adding, "Fine! Frostbite can stay for one more day!"

Alex was in a cheerful mood the whole day. The Legends had no need for their disguises now, so they found Willow eyeing them weirdly. Twylar was much content now, with one of the most important ingredients needed for the Cursed Blue gone. She didn't think 'The Great War' would happen at all! She stared at the cloudless sky peacefully. What was the point of all those countries signing up for a war that didn't even start? What good was it to join a war, if that would mean more suffering for your country?

Alex couldn't resist the charm of Frostbite's playful nature. As he gently tugged on the dragon's tail, Frostbite responded with a soft growl and a flick of its tail, sending Alex sprawling onto the ground with a laugh. The two wrestled and tumbled across the meadow, Alex's laughter mingling with Frostbite's low rumbling purrs. Their bond grew stronger with each playful tussle, a testament to the dragon's loyalty and the boy's unyielding spirit. Frostbite's scales shimmered in the sunlight, each movement revealing a spectrum of icy hues that fascinated Alex. They chased each other around the meadow, Frostbite occasionally lifting off the ground to hover playfully above Alex before swooping down again. This game of chase filled Alex's heart with joy and a sense of freedom he hadn't felt in a long time.

Meanwhile, in the cosy kitchen of the hideout, Moon and Estella busied themselves with the delightful task of baking an apple pie. The scent of fresh apples, cinnamon, and warm spices filled the air, creating an inviting atmosphere. Their hands moved in perfect harmony, slicing apples, mixing ingredients, and rolling out dough for their famous apple pie. Estella hummed a soft tune as she sprinkled cinnamon over the apple mixture while Moon carefully crimped the edges of the pie crust. The two worked in perfect sync, their laughter and chatter creating a comforting backdrop to the delicious aroma wafting through the room. Moon recounted a funny story from their recent adventures, causing Estella to giggle as she deftly peeled and cored the apples. As the pie was baked in the oven, they prepared a pot of tea, setting the table with care. The anticipation of sharing their culinary creation added an extra layer of warmth to the scene.

Out in the training grounds, Zilas and Ava sparred energetically, their movements fluid and precise as they practised their combat skills. The sound of clashing swords echoed around them, interspersed with bursts of cheerful banter. Zilas' eyes sparkled with mischief as he launched a surprise attack, which Ava deftly countered with a swift parry. Their training session was a blend of fierce concentration and friendly rivalry, each pushing the other to new heights of skill and strength. Zilas admired Ava's agility and quick reflexes, while Ava respected Zilas' strategic mind and powerful strikes. They took short breaks between bouts, sharing tips and techniques, and their camaraderie grew with each exchange. The sun cast long shadows on the training ground, but neither seemed to tire, driven by their shared goal of becoming stronger together.

Lily and Twylar lay side by side on the soft grass, their eyes fixed on the cloudless sky above. The tranquillity of the moment enveloped them, a stark contrast to the chaos they had faced. "Do you ever wonder what it would be like if none of this had happened?" Lily mused, her voice barely above a whisper. Twylar sighed softly, "Sometimes. But then I remember that every moment, everything we've gone through has led us to this point." They fell into a comfortable silence, finding peace in each other's presence and the endless expanse of the sky. The bright sun smiled warmly at the Earth. Alex found himself yet again telling the story of how he and Twylar managed to get hold of the Demon Lord's sceptre. The grass beneath them was cool and soft, and the faint hum of cicadas added to the peaceful ambience. They stayed there for hours, simply enjoying the quiet companionship and the beauty of the world around them.

Everything was going to be fine.